THE SOW'S EAR

A PAISLEY STERLING MYSTERY

THE SOW'S EAR

A PAISLEY STERLING MYSTERY

E. JOAN SIMS

WILDSIDE PRESS

CHAPTER ONE

One August afternoon shortly after her birthday, my handsome old broad of a mother and I had a heated exchange of words.

"I'm sick and tired of your complaints about growing older," I said.

She countered by pointing out that she was now attending more funerals than weddings. Never mind that she had just beat me soundly at tennis and still had enough energy to join my daughter Cassandra for a swim while I, a good eighteen years her junior, was still panting and sweating like a grampus—my pride the only thing keeping me in an upright position.

Anna Howard Sterling, nattily attired in her trim size-six swim suit and matching chiffon parau, had the last word when she left the women's locker room of the Rowan Springs Country Club in a graceful and elegant huff.

As soon as she was gone, I sprawled face-down on a wooden bench and gave in to exhaustion. As tiny silver stars shot up into my brain and burst into an artful display of fireworks behind my eyelids, I wondered if I were having a stroke. At that moment, I really could have cared less—and I would have killed for an icy cold gin-and-tonic.

I was just about to call on whatever hidden reserves of energy I had to get me to my feet and into the shower when I heard the locker room door open again.

Attempting to hide my red and sweating face, I struggled to a sitting position and bent over, pretending to untie my sneakers. Fortunately, the two women who entered were so engrossed in their conversation they didn't even notice me.

After they passed, I rested my head on my knees and let the sweat roll in a steady stream from my forehead to the end of my nose, watching in a zombie-like trance as drops gathered gathered and fell to the concrete floor—until I heard something that penetrated my mental haze.

"Do you really think he murdered her?"

"I tell you, Crystal, she'd never been sick a day in her life! The woman was a walking, talking, medical miracle. Winston used to say if everyone in Rowan Springs were as healthy as Millicent Grazziani, he would have to hang his shingle out somewhere else."

"But, murder, Agnes? Isn't that going a bit too far? Do you really think that puny little guy could get up enough gumption to kill somebody?" Crystal's laugh was rich and boisterous. "I remember when he was working as a hairdresser in Mildred's Beauty Box—that's how he met Millicent in the first place—he used to go to her house and do her hair twice a week. You could have knocked me over with a straw when he moved in with her. The story was that Millicent hated him. Used to tease him all the time. Called him 'Willie the wimp.'"

"People are funny," agreed Agnes. "Rich eccentric little old ladies included."

"Well, there's nothing funny about being the sole heir to one rich, eccentric little old lady's estate. Especially when she kicks the bucket under suspicious circumstances! I bet the grand jury…"

As their voices faded under the sound of the showers I hurriedly stuffed my tennis racket and clothes in a bag and headed for my car. Mother had come in her own brand new baby blue Continental. She could give Cass a lift home.

I had no idea who "Crystal" was, but I was well acquainted with her friend, and I definitely wanted to avoid a meeting. Agnes Wallace was the on-again, off-again ex-wife of a local doctor. From the look of me, it would be an easy assumption that I was about to suffer a heart attack. Gabby little Agnes would delight in spreading the sad news all over town, and my obituary would be in the newspaper before anyone thought to call me up and confirm my passing.

It was the last day of summer—a beautiful "store-bought" day, with brilliant blue skies and temperatures hovering in the nineties. I stopped by the drive-in window at the Dairy Queen for two large iced teas and two cups of iced water to go. After the initial shock, the cup of cold water between my knees felt wonderful, as did the ice cubes in my sports bra. As I cruised down Main Street with the air conditioner on high, I began to feel a bit more human.

Several years ago, Millicent Grazziani decided to build an imposing residence next to the bank that her late husband had owned. The local businessmen screamed "zoning violation," but the dear lady dug in her elegant little heels and stuck out her tongue at the city council. Three months later, her townhouse as well as the bank on Main Street mysteriously burned down in the middle of the night. Her two beloved poodles and several hundred thousand dollars worth of priceless antiques went up in hungry scarlet flames that could be seen for miles.

Millicent was royally pissed and absolutely refused to allow the bank to be rebuilt. Instead, she donated the blackened rectangle of land between the Rite-Med Pharmacy and Hinkle's Dry Goods to the town as a park. She also donated a sizeable trust fund for the maintenance of the property. The gift was so generous that the people of Rowan Springs chose to overlook the fact that the park was dedicated to Peachy Keen and Pinky Grazziani and sported their little likenesses carved in imported Italian marble at the entrance. They even went so far as to overlook the fact that Pinky was quite obviously relieving himself against the handsome wrought-iron gate.

I thought it was a hoot and took my hat off to Madame Grazziani. What was money for if it couldn't buy you the last word? I usually smiled as I passed the park entrance and saw the life-sized statues of the playful little poodles, but today there was a huge white bow of mourning tied to the gate, and the stone dogs seemed cold and dead and very much alone.

By the time I arrived at my mother's sprawling country home on Meadowdale Farm, I had recovered enough to go for a short romp with our—make that, Cassie's—dog, Agatha Christie. Aggie was a wild and wooly little Lhasa Apso with the face of a fuzzy white angel and the temperament of a cobra. I wore myself out all over again, and by the time I got in the shower, it was all I could do not to collapse under the spray of the water. It would be a shame to avoid a heart attack and then drown in the bathtub.

I was sitting on the big screened-in back porch sipping a glass of *chenin blanc* and drying my unruly auburn curls in the last rays of the afternoon sun when Mother and Cassie drove up in the driveway. Mother's brand new husband, Horatio Raleigh, pulled up right behind them in his gunmetal gray Bentley.

Mother hopped out of her car with the agility of a sixteen year-old and went to meet Horatio. Her hand on his arm, they followed Cassie up the walk and paused to admire Aggie who was performing one of her welcoming dances for everyone's approval.

"Mom," asked Cassie, "where did you disappear? We looked all over the club. And then Agnes Wallace told us she saw you in the parking lot from the window in the locker room. She said you looked kind of funny and to be sure and call Winston if you needed anything."

"Yeah, in a pig's eye!" I still had some serious problems trusting Winston Wallace's medical acumen.

"She told us some other very sad news, Paisley, dear."

"Yes, I know, Mother. Millicent Grazziani is dead. She may have been murdered—and there's a big white bow on the park entrance."

Mother looked deflated. It was the first time that day I had beaten her to the punch. I smiled all the way down to my gizzard.

"Ah, Paisley, what would we do without you to set us all straight?" Horatio laughed softly.

"Yeah, Mom, you do cut to the chase. What do you think, Horatio? You knew Mrs. Grazziani. Do you think someone killed her?"

Horatio shook his handsome white head as he poured glasses of wine for himself and Mother.

"Who knows, my child? A decade ago, I would have denied that anyone in our fair city could commit a violent crime, but the last few years have proved me wrong. And since our Paisley has taken to writing mystery novels instead of children's books, I have noticed an increasing amount of evil in our midst."

"That's it Mom," Cassie said. "Because you took the *nom de plume* of Leonard Paisley and chucked Aunty Jenny and *Bartholomew the Blue-eyed Cricket*, we're having a crime wave."

"I knew somehow it would have to be my fault," I grumbled.

"You must admit that we have had more than our fair share of excitement since you and that dreadful Leonard started the detective business, dear," Mother said.

"I don't know about that," I said. "You had some pretty exciting adventures when you traveled with Dad, and Cassie and I lived through a South American revolution. Horatio, I'm sure you had some high old times when you were in Europe. I've even heard it whispered that you did some undercover work for the CIA. You must have seen your share of excitement doing that."

"There you go again, my dear," he said. "You must be careful not to repeat these creative fantasies in front of people who might believe you." He smiled benevolently, but under that handsome roguish forehead his bright eyes twinkled with mischief. I wasn't just spinning tales and he and I both knew it.

"At any rate," he continued, "it would appear as though Paisley may be right. We've all experienced violence before. Perhaps it's not the number of violent crimes that has changed, but our ability to find out about them so rapidly. The inventions of modern man have made the ends of the Earth easier to reach. What happens in Melbourne tonight will be splashed across the morning newspaper instead of arriving in the mail packet of a sailing ship in three months time."

"Just one thing, Horatio," said Cassie. "This is not exactly a big wicked city. Rowan Springs is only a quaint, sleepy little southern town, population eight thousand five hundred."

"Exactly, my child. Eight thousand five hundred human beings with human passions and frailties—each and every one capable of violence under the right circumstances."

"I know what happened to the old lady," my voice sounding as lazy and relaxed as I felt.

"What, Paisley, dear?" asked Mother.

"She had a really bad hair day."

I smiled, ignoring their groans. I loved bad jokes—and the darker, the better.

CHAPTER TWO

I slept like a log that night—at least, until three in the morning when an owl in the wild cherry tree down by the carriage house decided it was a good time to shout his amorous intentions to any female within hooting distance.

After forty-five minutes of tossing, turning, and trying to breathe with my head under the pillow, I finally admitted that I was licked and got out of bed. I threw on some jeans and a faded old Atlanta Braves sweatshirt—the one with the autograph of my favorite player on the hem—and tiptoed into the library. After quietly opening the French doors, I sat cross-legged on the floor in front of the screen and listened to the lonesome owl.

At first I was amused as I imagined this relatively unappealing creature with his big yellow eyes and pointy beak crying out for love and affection. Then, quite suddenly, I realized I was crying. Before long, big old sobs wrenched their way up out of my chest, and I cried as though my heart were broken. Ten minutes later I was on the hiccoughy end of my crying jag, and searching around in the dark for a box of tissues.

I finally gave up looking and groped my way into the bathroom. I blew my nose on some toilet paper and splashed cold water on my eyes in the vain hope that tomorrow they wouldn't be swollen and puffy. As I dried off with my bath towel I glanced out the window and saw a figure crossing out of the shadows under the owl's tree to the carriage house.

I opened the screen door as quietly as I could and slipped out. When I stepped in the dew-wet grass I realized I had forgotten my shoes. I knew that I would lose sight of the intruder if I went back so I crossed quickly over the gravel driveway lifting my feet up comically as the tiny rocks dug painfully into the soft flesh of my insteps. I made it to the orchard just as my quarry disappeared around the corner where Mother's new car was parked right next to Horatio's.

Ah, ha! I thought, a car thief. And I had caught him red-handed. Me! All by myself!

I raced to the corner of the building and jumped out shouting.

"The jig's up! Come out and fight like a man!"

"Oh, Mom, for Pete's sake!"

"Cassie! What in the hell are you doing out here in the middle of the night?"

"The same thing as you, I imagine. Listening to that poor lonely old hooty owl and crying like a baby."

"How did you know?"

"I heard you when I walked around from the back porch." She came over and hugged me. "Are you okay now?"

I shrugged, and then shivered a bit. After the heat of the day, the night air felt cool and my feet were wet.

"Yeah, I'm fine. I don't know what came over me."

"Loneliness. It happens to the best of us."

We walked slowly—arm in arm—back up toward the house.

"Guess so," I admitted. I just thought I was over all that."

"You mean missing Daddy?"

"My God, Cassie, it's been years since he disappeared."

"You loved him very much. And you never really knew what happened to him. That's enough to give anybody nightmares. San Romero in those last few days was enough to give me nightmares for years, and I was just a little kid. But I remember."

"Do you, Cassie? I tried to make everything seem as normal as possible for you."

"Even a little child knows something is terribly wrong when her Daddy goes to the jungle and doesn't come back—when Mommy has to sneak us out of the country in the dead of night and leave all my dolls behind—not to mention my Daddy."

"I'm so sorry, sugar." I squeezed her hand.

"Me, too, Mom. Sorry for you, I mean." She squeezed me back. "I know you must have missed him terribly those first few years in New York. Why didn't you ever find a nice man to share your life with? Was it because of me?"

I laughed. "You forget. We were living with Pam. You know her preferences. We were surrounded by women!"

Cassie joined in my laughter and soon we were happily reminiscing about the "good old" bad old days when we lived with the woman who had been my college roommate.

Pamela Alison Winslow was now my agent and still my best friend. She was the one to suggest that I write down some of the bedtime stories I made up for Cassie. She had helped me establish a career when I arrived on her doorstep without a dime to my name and a little girl to support.

I could have gone home to my parents but I wanted to come back on my own terms. I had something to prove. I had been the spoiled daughter of well-to-do parents and the pampered wife of a wealthy foreign diplomat. I had never been a responsible adult taking care of my child alone. With Pam's help and wise editorial guidance I achieved my goal.

For almost a decade I enjoyed a certain amount of popularity as "Aunty Jenny." There was even talk of a television special. Then gradually *Bartholomew the Blue-eyed Cricket* dropped in popularity, and when my last kiddy book didn't sell, Pam urged me to find another *genre*. I started writing hard-boiled detective stories, and Leonard Paisley was born.

At first, I resented having to share my literary fame with the non-existent hero of my novels, but Pam kept assuring me it was "good for business." She also said nobody would take a freckled-faced, green-eyed housewife and mother seriously when it came to murder and mayhem. After all, the most violent act I had ever committed was tearing up my panty hose when I came back to live on the farm.

I had thought I was happy. What was wrong with me?

Cassie made hot chocolate with tons of marshmallows while I washed and dried my feet. We turned the gas logs in my bedroom on low and sat in front of the fireplace toasting extra marshmallows over the flames.

"So, are you going to write about Mrs. Grazziani?"

I laughed. Cassie could always read my mind. "Sure. Why not? She deserves to live on in posterity. I always admired the old bag. She had panache."

I swallowed the crusty burnt shell of marshmallow and licked my fingers. "She was a kleptomaniac. Did you know that?"

"Oh, Mom, you kidding. That old lady had more money than God. Why on Earth would she steal anything?"

"For the thrill of it, I suppose. Anyway, when she used to go to Chicago every fall people would joke, 'Millicent's gone Christmas shoplifting!' They say she had special skirts made with pockets that had slits so she could swipe stuff and hang it on a belt under her waist."

"Did she ever get caught?"

"Only once. All the stores here in town knew what she was doing, but no one ever said a thing. Her husband would go around each month and pay for what she took. Then one fine day the Five and Dime got a new manager. He saw her swiping a bottle of *Evening in Paris* cologne and called the police. He insisted that she be arrested."

"Was she?"

"You'll have to ask Gran exactly what the details were. All I know is that the dime store had another new manager the next week, and Millicent never spent a night in jail. Her husband was very rich and powerful. Nobody wanted to have him for an enemy."

"Little town politics."

"You got that right! Tony Grazziani donated the money for the new high school gymnasium, the gazebo grandstand at Big Springs Park, and half the fire trucks in Lakeland County."

Cassie laughed merrily. "Which at the time must have been one!"

"Right!"

Cassie burped. "I wish I hadn't eaten those last three marshmallows."

"Let's go to bed. You'll feel fine in the morning. You have youth and beauty on your side. I, on the other hand, will have bags under my eyes big enough to store half my wardrobe."

Cassie got up from the floor in one graceful motion. I pulled half the covers off the bed in my struggle to get to my feet.

"Mom, you have to start jogging with me again. You were in such great shape six months ago. What happened?"

"Leonard's latest, that's what. Sitting on your butt ten hours a day doesn't do much for the figure."

"Let's start tomorrow morning at...."

She looked at my raised eyebrow and smiled.

"Tomorrow evening when it gets cooler will be great." She bent over from her height, which was four inches above my five feet six and gave me a good night kiss.

"Love you, Mom."

"Me, too, Cassie. Sleep tight."

I closed the door behind her and went back into the library to lock the French doors.

A faint pink tinge hovered over the horizon. It was almost dawn. The morning birds were beginning to wake up and sing their welcome to the sun. It was time for me and the lonesome owl to go to bed.

CHAPTER THREE

I forgot about Mother's hen party until I got up late the next morning and stumbled into the kitchen for breakfast. Plates of dainty finger sandwiches, iced and decorated *petit fours*, tiny biscuits with country ham, and jam-filled teacakes covered every available countertop. The creator of this culinary magic was seated at the big country kitchen table hulling strawberries.

"My lord, Mother! Just how much food can a bunch of little old biddies eat?"

"You'd be surprised, Paisley, dear," she answered with a smile. "And besides, some of them like to take a little snack home for later."

I sneaked a strawberry while she wasn't looking and poured myself a cup of hot tea. "Got anything you can spare for your poor starving offspring?"

She cast an appraising eye over the excess of gourmet goodies. "There's a container of broken biscuits and ham silvers in the refrigerator. You can finish whatever Cassie left. She practically flew through here an hour ago on her way to the animal clinic."

"Aggie under the weather?" I asked, adding, "One can only hope," under my breath.

"No, thank goodness. The groomer had an unexpected opening and so the puppy's having her hair clipped."

"Wish they'd file down her teeth," I grumbled.

"What's that, dear?" asked Mother. "By the way, Paisley," she continued without waiting for my answer. "Thank you so much for helping me serve luncheon."

"What? I never said…"

"I know you didn't, dear, but when Mable called and said her youngest wasn't feeling well, I knew you would want to jump right in and volunteer."

"But, but…"

"Thanks again, darling," she insisted firmly.

"What about Cassie? Can't she…"

She turned and gave me a warning glance. "And please do something about your hair. We don't want stray red curls in our fresh shrimp salad, now do we?"

"Shrimp salad?" She knew that was my favorite. "Where are you hiding it?"

"And do wear something nice, dear. I want to show off my beautiful daughter."

"Then call Velvet and tell her to get her fancy little butt over here to prance around in the latest Chanel."

"Anything but jeans and those dreadful moccasins, dear. And you know perfectly well that Velvet is in Mykonos with…with her new husband."

"Ah, ha! You can't remember his name either! How many husbands has my dear sister had now? Four? Five?"

"Anthony," she decided. "It's Anthony, or Alexander. One or the other—I'm almost positive. And don't be ugly, dear. It's so unbecoming the way you prattle on about Velvet's romantic foibles."

"Foibles, *foibles*? And what about marriage vows, Mother? What about forever?"

"We can only hope she's found the right one, dear. She's positive she has,…well, almost positive, anyway. And don't forget, dear, no jeans."

Mother's fiesta went off without a hitch, unless you count my accidentally dumping a plateful of shortbread cookies in the ample lap of a jolly lady who grabbed as many as she could and stuffed them in her pocketbook before I could come back with the broom.

By the time the last car left the driveway and the last flower-bedecked little hat bobbed out of sight, I was exhausted. My cheeks ached from the smile plastered on my face, and my pinched toes screamed in agony. I kicked off the dress-up shoes my mother had forced me to wear and grabbed a bottle of Australian *Riesling* from the refrigerator. The shrimp salad had disappeared before I even got to taste it, so I settled for a plate of fruit and cheese and headed out to the patio just as Horatio drove up in his Bentley.

"Afternoon, my dear," he said with a smile on his tanned aristocratic face. "One might surmise from that sour look that even though your mother's extravaganza was a complete success, you are not in the best of moods."

"You got that right!"

"And by the way, you look very nice, my dear, even barefoot. I sometimes forget how truly lovely you are."

"Yeah, yeah," I grumbled, but I couldn't help enjoying the affirmation. It had been a

long time since a man had paid me a compliment.

"I thought you'd be busy arranging Madame Grazziani's wake," I asked to change the subject and cover my embarrassment. Horatio was the owner of our town's one and only funeral home. He had passed most of the responsibility of day-to-day management on to his nephew, but when someone of note or fortune passed to the great beyond, Horatio usually was the one who made all of the arrangements. His taste was impeccable and his august presence leant an air of elegance to even the most dismal of occasions.

He shook his head and frowned ever so slightly. "That has me puzzled, my child. I had, of course, expected that she would make that stipulation in her last wishes, but young Hawkins, her lawyer, called me this morning after her will was read and told me Millicent wanted to be cremated without further ado."

"And no wake, no funeral, no nothing? But, I thought…"

He smiled. "You've heard the coffin story, too, I suppose."

"Of course," I laughed.

"Well, it is true that she came in five years ago and ordered the most expensive casket on the market. I, too, was aghast when I found out she was using it for a coffee table," he chuckled.

"You gotta admit, it makes for a great storyline. I used it in *Dead Bones and Bloody Bodies*.

"My goodness, Paisley! Our Leonard is a lurid fellow!"

"That he is," I agreed with a clownish grin.

I heard the screen door to the porch close and Mother's footsteps on the walkway. I leaned in closer to whisper, "Please don't mention that you like my outfit to Mother. I don't want her to think…"

"Don't want me to think what, dear?" asked Mother as Horatio rose to offer her a seat.

"How much it would disturb you to know our late friend Millicent did not want us to join in communion to offer our last condolences," said Horatio.

"That's definitely not what Paisley said," laughed Mother. "But considering how much work she did today, I'll let it pass. And that really is astonishing news, Horatio. I would have assumed the dear old thing would have wanted an extravagant affair to mark her passing."

Mother had brought two more wine glasses. I filled them while Horatio told her about the Millicent's will.

He finished with, "And the 'coffee table'—I guess he inherits that along with the house and all of her antiques."

"Wait just a darn minute! He, who? Billy—her hairdresser?"

"Paisley!"

Horatio laughed and took a sip of the chilled wine. "Where did you hear that, my dear?"

The country club—yesterday afternoon, from Agnes Wallace and her friend, what's-her-name."

"Ah, locker room gossip, I presume."

"Yep! And they also said he murdered her."

"For goodness sake, Paisley. You shouldn't repeat something as tacky as that!"

"Now, now, Anna, Paisley is simply stating what's on everyone else's lips. And from what I understand there may be something to the accusation, considering the arguments the two of them used to have in public."

"Ohhh, do tell us more, Horatio. Sounds like a good story."

"Paisley, common gossip is quite unbecoming of southern lady."

"Oh, Mother! Give me a break! Remember, I served luncheon to fourteen little blabbermouths with twenty-eight eager ears this afternoon. Don't think I don't know what their favorite pastime is. Sunday school class, my hind foot!"

"Horatio," she said, casting an icy glance in my direction. "I put some lovely shrimp salad aside for you. When you're ready to eat, join me in the kitchen where it's not so hot and unpleasant."

Horatio barely managed to smother a chuckle when I stuck my tongue out at her retreating and totally disapproving back.

"Now!" I said, as I topped off our wine glasses and winked at my friend, "What arguments?"

CHAPTER FOUR

Billy Arlequin and Millicient Grazziani had fought frequently and very publicly—too many times for Horatio to remember. They had arguments over money, cars, clothes, when and where to eat, and Millicent's health. Some of their worst battles had taken place at her doctor's office and had been broadcast by the receptionist who, because of all the secrets she knew, enjoyed a certain level of fearful respect in Rowan Springs. She had once confided to Horatio's nephew that Billy had walked out and left Millicent with no way to get home except the town's one and only taxi. And this was after screaming, "I hate you—you hideous old hag!" at the top of his lungs in the waiting room.

When Billy had called the police department and had the old woman's driver's license revoked on her last birthday, Millicent had gotten behind the wheel of her ancient Silver Cloud and chased him through the neighborhood—uprooting shrubs, destroying flowerbeds, and ending up with a cracked and smoking radiator against the trunk of a big oak tree. Billy had escaped without a scratch except for his bruised dignity, but the neighbors who had gathered to watch reported later that he had sworn he would "get even with the bitch."

"So you think he killed her" I asked, as he rose in preparation to join Mother in the kitchen.

"You should hardly jump to that conclusion, my dear. After all, these things were said in anger—something we all do every day."

"We? Do you shout at people every day, Horatio? I don't, even though I'd love to strangle Mother right about now. She's teased me with that shrimp salad all day long. I feel like Pavlov's drooling canine."

"Speaking of canines—where has your mother hidden Cassie's resident beastie? I assume she wasn't invited to the party?"

"To be honest, I don't know. Cassie took her to the groomer's this morning and they've both been gone all day."

"Then I know where they are," he stated with a knowing smile. "There's a new vet in town—Dr. Huntley Haverstock. He's working on a joint project with the university extension service—something to do with the "hoof and mouth" epidemic in the British Isles."

"A Brit?"

"A very handsome young Brit, if I do say so. I met him at a Chamber of Commerce luncheon. I must admit I would have informed Cassandra of the new blood right away, if it hadn't been for…"

I laughed. "What's he got? Two heads?"

Horatio chuckled along with me, "No, but he's at least one head shorter than our dear Cassandra."

Cassie came home shortly after Horatio joined Mother in the kitchen to feast on my shrimp salad. Aggie bounded out of the car and ran to my side, eager to show off her new hairdo. I "ohhed' and "ahhed" appreciatively, and reached down to pat the soft fluffy fur. I just managed to jerk my hand back in time to avoid a vicious nip.

"You rotten little…"

"Doesn't she look adorable?" called Cassie.

My daughter was a beauty, all right. I admired the glossy straight brown hair and the ivory oval of that perfect face as she cross the grassy expanse of yard to reach me. Her legs were long, tanned and slender, and her figure firm and athletic; but her best feature was the total lack of awareness of her natural good looks. She was a true American beauty—North and South.

"Trish took special care with her today."

"Meaning that she wore her stainless steel gauntlets?"

"Mom, don't be mean! Aggie has never bitten Trish."

"How about Patty, and Maud, and what's-her-name—the one from Cincinnati."

"They…they were not as professional as Trish," stammered Cassie. "And Aggie could tell. They made her nervous."

I slid back down in the chaise with a smirk on my face. "So, when's the big date with the little vet?"

"Ohhhh! You can be soooo…I'm in a hurry, or I would…"

The two of them—dog and daughter—managed to portray the same amount of disdain as they tossed their heads and marched off towards the house. I laughed again and poured myself another glass of wine. Cassie and I had been home for just a little over three years, and yet she had worked her way through almost all the eligible bachelors in Rowan Springs. There weren't that many—true, but they didn't last long either. She had gotten really mad at me last summer when I asked her if she wanted us to install a revolving door.

The evening was soft and beautiful—with that quiet majesty that accompanies approaching twilight. Across the wide horizon, the sky deepened to orange and red, then blue and purple, and objects in the distance could be seen with increasing clarity as the dust settled.

I loved this time of the day and eagerly awaited that one majestic moment when the sun sinks below the tree line and the stars make their first appearance in the deep blue of the heavens. I breathed a sigh of contentment as Venus came into view, and quietly thanked God once again for allowing me to come home to Meadowdale Farm.

Sometimes, admittedly, I missed the hustle and bustle of our busy lives in Manhattan—mostly when I had a yearning for a really fresh bagel. And certainly, if I allowed myself to think about it, I missed our happy life in San Romero; but I had resigned myself to being alone, just as Mother had until quite recently. I was fairly certain that, unlike her, I would never marry again. With few exceptions, the only men in my life were "Leonard" and his nefarious henchmen—and that was only when I sat down at my father's desk to work on a book.

Horatio had to call my name twice, and was almost at my side before I shook off my musing. "Wha…what did you say?"

"My nephew has called from the, er, office. Someone made a mistake and started to embalm Madame Grazziani. Thank heaven Archibald stopped them in time, but not before something very disturbing was uncovered."

"What?" I repeated again—parrot fashion.

"I'm not sure, my dear. But I think you may want to come along with me. From poor Archie's babbling, I think it may be something grisly enough for one for your books."

CHAPTER FIVE

This wasn't the first time I had been to Horatio's place of business, but it was the first time I had ever been invited to view a body. Despite my repeated hints that Leonard needed to do some research, Horatio had steadfastly refused to allow me within the confines of the clinical end of his enterprise until now. I was surprised to discover that my first impression was a reminder of "Biology 101" and the infamous frog dissection. The place reeked of formaldehyde and other noxious odors. When I asked how he was able to keep the stench away from the quiet elegance of the public rooms, Horatio pointed to several large air ducts scattered about the suspended ceiling.

"Forced air system," he answered abruptly.

In this place of death, Horatio seemed different: quiet and determined—as though he had hung his debonair *persona* on the coat rack in the hall along with his natty umbrella. I fell in with his solemn mood and kept the rest of my inane questions to myself.

Horatio's nephew had other business to attend to and had therefore left the mortal remains of Millicent Grazziani alone in the mortuary. With a quiet reverence, Horatio approached the long stainless steel table where she lay, pausing for a moment before he lifted the pristine white sheet to look into her sightless eyes. He smiled gently—inexplicably, as if in apologetic greeting and then pulled the fabric back below her waist. My startled gasp echoed against the white tile walls of the laboratory and triggered the little response in my nervous system that makes your goose bumps rise.

"What the hell is that?"

Horatio frowned briefly at my lack of sensitivity and took his time examining the skin of Millicent's scarred and damaged abdomen before he answered.

"I can't be sure, of course, and I hate to make such an assumption because of the psychological ramifications and the social stigma attached…"

"Horatio," I blurted, "is that what I think it is?"

He sighed, a sad and gentle sigh. "Yes, Paisley, I fear our Millicent practiced self-mutilation, probably because of some deep-seated and unresolved problems from childhood. I've read about it, but this is the first time I've had occasion to see it for myself. Poor, dear Millicent, what pain she must have endured. Some of these scars are very old. She must have started cutting herself at a very early age."

"Sick! It's just sick! Yuck!"

Horatio looked up, and I could read the sorrow in his eyes. It was something I had never seen before. I realized for the first time why he had gladly turned over the business to his nephew. He must have seen the physical remnants of many tragedies in his time. For a moment his solemn gaze chided me without words before he responded.

"When you get to be my age, my dear, perhaps you'll be more reluctant to pass judgment on the frailties of others."

"How did she do it, do you think?" I asked in a whisper. "Pen knife, potato peeler, or what?"

Horatio managed a tiny smile. "Certainly not a potato peeler. Something, I think, with a very sharp point—something used over and over again until these deep marks were made."

"Damnation! It must have hurt like a bitch!"

"Somewhat inelegantly put—but quite true nonetheless. The pain must have been considerable, but I imagine that was part and parcel of the whole package."

"Her dementia, you mean?"

"The Millicent Grazziani I knew was not suffering from dementia. She was eccentric, possibly—no, probably—very immature, selfish and certainly neurotic—but not crazy."

"Then why the tic-tac-toe on her tummy?"

"Self-mutilation is usually an act of self-punishment—brought on by an overwhelming sense of guilt. Although some mental specialists think that it's caused by a desire to feel something—anything, by women, who have sublimated their feelings because of some severe emotional trauma in the past."

I leaned in closer to examine the ugly network of scars. "Women?"

"Almost always."

"Looks like letters."

"I doubt it, Paisley. That doesn't fit the pattern."

"Pattern, smattern! Look at this one. That's either an 'm' or a 'w.'"

Horatio adjusted the overhead light as I pointed to the vertical lines surrounding Millicent's wrinkled navel.

"Humm." He walked away from the circle of bright light for a moment and came back with a large magnifying glass with a wide metal rim. He held it this way and that trying to focus on the confluent lines without touching the old woman's skin.

"Look, you've got to pull her skin out so it's smooth and then you can see it better." I reached out, but he grabbed my hand before I touched the body.

"Wait!" he commanded. "Don't ever touch a corpse without putting on gloves."

"Wow! That's a bit of wisdom I'll store away," I laughed nervously. "Just hope I don't have to unpack it very often."

Horatio handed the magnifying glass to me as he turned around to find the box of latex gloves. As the glass passed underneath the light I caught a momentary glimpse of something odd reflected in the metal rim.

"Horatio do you have a mirror handy?"

He turned, puzzled, a slight frown on his face. "She's quite dead, I assure you. No need to hold a mirror under her nose."

"Nah, it's not that. I just thought I saw something strange." I held the metal rim over the pale sagging tissue of what was once a young and vibrant body and saw it again.

"Words!" I stammered. "She used her skin for a notepad!"

Horatio wheeled around as he handed me the gloves. "Coincidence," he guessed. "Nothing more than sheer happenstance."

I tugged on the gloves and pushed my unruly hair out of my eyes. "I don't think so. These marks were deliberate—deep and repetitive. You said so yourself." The goose bumps on my own arms tingled with repulsion as I reached down and pulled carefully upwards on the loose abdominal skin. I was rewarded immediately for my efforts as the markings took on a whole new look.

"There is a pattern," I said. My voice sounded faint and shocked even to me. "Find me a mirror and I'll prove it to you."

A discrete knock and a quiet voice interrupted us. Horatio turned and nodded as one of his white-coated assistants beckoned from the doorway.

"Have to go, my dear. The ambulance is here from Nashville to take Millicent to the crematorium. There are some forms I need to sign. I hate to ask, but can you find your way out? That door," he said pointing to the opposite wall, "leads directly to the parking lot."

"But,…but…"

"I'm truly sorry to spoil your Sherlockian moment, Paisley, but I don't have a mirror in here. There's hardly a reason for one, and besides, I'm afraid we differ on the nature of poor Millicent's injuries." He turned and fixed me with a solemn look. "You must promise me that what we have seen will not be broadcast through-out the community. This," he said, pointing at Millicent's bare midriff, "is obviously the reason she chose to be cremated. Our accidental discovery of her secret must remain our secret as well. That means Leonard must never find out," he added sternly.

"Of course, Horatio!" I replied, earnestly. "I wouldn't dare to… but how about a camera? Could we take some pictures and figure it out later? Just the two of us—on the QT of course!"

Horatio shrugged off his lab coat and slipped on his impeccably tailored grey pinstriped suit jacket before he turned to me with a slight smile on his face. "I know I can trust you, my child, but sometimes you are incorrigible. As for the photographs, we do not have permission from the next-of-kin for that sort of nonsense."

"But there is no next-of-kin!" I protested. His only answer was the square and determined set to his retreating shoulders.

Cassie had left a disposable camera in the glove case of my car the last time we went for a drive to the lake. I was sure there was enough film left because an unexpected rain shower had cut our trip short. The question that remained was—did I have enough time to grab the camera and take the pictures before Horatio returned?

I hurried to the big double doors and peered out from between the heavy vinyl blinds. The ambulance driver was leaning casually against the hearse. When he pulled a pack of cigarettes out of his pocket and lit one, I decided to give it a try.

The double doors were heavy and the forced air from the ventilator system made them seem even heavier as I pushed them open. I pulled off my moccasin and stuck it between them so they wouldn't close all the way and lock me out, and dashed across the parking lot wincing with pain as the asphalt—still holding heat from the sun—punished my one barefoot. I grabbed the camera from the glove compartment and ran back across the parking lot and inside the morgue without even retrieving my shoe.

The little camera had no flash, but fortunately the bright lights over the examining table were more than satisfactory. Remembering Horatio's concern for Millicent's sensibilities, I was careful to cover everything but the area of stomach, abdomen, and midriff where the skin was scarred and mutilated. Running around the table like a mad terrier, I took shots from several directions. When I heard the engine of the ambulance start up, I figured my time was up and dashed back over to the door—returning to pull the white sheet back up over Millicent's body just in the nick of time.

The ambulance driver was backing slowly up to the double doors when I shot out like a bullet and slammed against the side of his polished fender. Ignoring his vehement oaths, I gave him a weak apologetic smile, slipped on my other shoe, and climbed in my car for a quick getaway. I looked over my shoulder just as the double doors opened all the way and one of Horatio's minions made ready to tuck Madame Grazziani in for her last ride.

Cackling gleefully, I congratulated myself as I drove out to the highway where the big convenience stores were. One of them was bound to have a speedy developing service. I could have my grisly little photographs in one hour.

The guilt didn't set in until I was almost settled in the perfect parking spot in front of the Save-Mart. Furiously I fought to sublimate my finer feelings. It didn't matter, I insisted to the devil within me, that Horatio was one of my best friends and had been in love with my mother for years. Who cared if he would gladly lay down his life for her, or Cassie, or even me? And the answer was—I cared. I cared a whole bunch. I sighed and tucked the camera back in the glove case along with my curiosity, then let a very grateful lady with an enormous black curly wig and too much eye makeup take my parking spot.

The Dairy Queen was on my way home, it was way past suppertime, and I was hungry despite the macabre exercise I had just participated in. I cheered up considerably as I contemplated the choice of cheeseburger versus slaw dog, then deciding that I had used enough will power in the last few minutes to last all week, I added a hot fudge sundae to my wish list.

CHAPTER SIX

It poured all day, every single day of the next week. Mother and Cassie were constantly engaged in their rainy-day argument about where and when Aggie was—as mother called it—to "relieve" herself. The squeamish little puppy adamantly refused to venture outside when the grass was wet. My sympathies were with the dog. Her little pink tummy was almost hairless and it was totally vulnerable when she squatted to pee.

I stayed out of the fray as I had many times before by pretending to be hard at work in the library. I did try to write, but my mind kept flipping back to the memory of another tummy—Millicent's wrinkled and ancient abdominal wall and the cryptic markings hidden in the folds of that fragile, almost transparent skin. I yearned to solve the mystery of those epidermal hieroglyphics and tried in vain to forget the forbidden camera in the glove case of my car—the camera that was loaded with the answers to all my questions.

I imagined how easy it would be to take the processed photos and scan them into my computer then zoom in on Millicent's scars. I could use the fancy software I had bought on a whim, to enlarge, shadow, highlight, or even turn inside out any suspicious areas. It would be so easy, so intriguing—and so much fun.

I got up from my father's big leather chair and chided myself for thinking about the entertainment I would derive from inspecting Millicent's ancient flesh under a microscope. I should be sorry that the frail little old lady was dead. What was I, a ghoul? Yes, I freely admitted to myself. Every mystery writer is a ghoul to some extent. We're the worst kind of rubber-neckers on the highway after an accident. We see evil in every motive and foul play in every tragedy. Our refrigerators have little magnets with daggers and pistols instead of muffin pans and jelly jars. And under those magnets, more often than not, are lists of undetectable poisons and different types of firearms. We're a bloodthirsty lot, no doubt about it, and I was one of the worst.

My "Leonard" was of the old school—a hard drinking, rowdy man's man who would collar his best friend, bed his wife, and snuff his parakeet, but never ever cheat at cards.

Leonard looked like the anti-hero on every *film noir* poster. He wore his fedora pulled down over his eyes and a cigarette on the edge of his lip. There was always a faint sneer on his face under the thin, ironic slash of a mustache, and his hair was on the wrong end of visit to the barber. He used Bogie's vocabulary, and solved Chandler's crimes. He was despised by every policeman and politician, and beloved by every waitress and hooker in Manhattan.

Mother very often forgot that he was fictitious and hated him with a passion—blaming him for my casual manner of dress and sometimes raw and colorful use of language. I had to remind her quite often that this wasn't a case of the chicken and the egg: I had indeed come first, and no matter how much she complained—as long as he paid the bills—Leonard wasn't going anywhere.

It was still raining outside and wasn't really very cold, but there was no denying the damp chill in the air. I punched the magic plunger on the gas logs in the big fireplace and watched as they burst into flames. It was something to behold. I shook my head in awe, thinking of all the winter evenings in the past when we had taken turns huffing and puffing over sticks of kindling and twisted bits of paper trying to coax them into a relatively decent fire. We had always spent a great deal of time in this room and my father had finally decided to have the gas logs installed. Too bad he died before he could really enjoy them.

I looked around at the photographs of family and friends—enjoying as I always did the feeling of being secure in my roots. Our family had been in Kentucky for generations. My great-great-great grandfather built the house that's serenaded at the Kentucky Derby every year. Some even swore that our first land grant came from the largess of none other than Catherine Parr, the last and most fortunate wife of Henry the Eighth. I didn't care how, or when—the *where* was the only thing that mattered to me. I loved this part of the world and never wanted to leave again. I had done that once—as a new bride—eager to plant my new husband and myself in another country far from home.

"I must'a been nuts!" I scoffed. But I knew the truth. I had been crazy—crazy in love—crazy enough to say goodbye to everything else that mattered to me and follow Rafe to the ends of the Earth. And just for the record—for the brief but beautiful time it lasted, it was worth it. Cassie was proof enough of that.

With some effort, I shook off the past and sat back down at the computer. My hands were poised over the keys and my mind struggling to form a sentence when the phone rang—saving me from the agony of coming up blank.

"Paisley?"

"Horatio?"

"Do we go on with the name game, my dear, or can we discuss something else now?"

I settled back and found a comfortable spot in the chair.

"You first," I laughed.

He sighed over the phone line, and I felt the first prickling of alarm. It was unusual for Horatio to show any signs of stress or defeat, yet he definitely sounded tired and worn.

"I should have taken your advice, Paisley dear," he admitted, sighing deeply once again.

"About what? I can't think of anything that I know more about than you."

"Millicent's scars. I should have let you photograph them. We might have been able to save a man from the electric chair."

"Billy?" I whispered hoarsely.

"Yes, my dear. Billy Arlequin has been arrested for Millicent's murder. He swears the scars on her abdomen are evidence to his innocence. I will never forgive myself for forbidding you to take those photographs." He chuckled ironically. "Too bad you're so respectful and obedient, my child."

"Uh, well, about that obedient part," I told him with a grin. "Maybe I have some good news for you."

There was a moment's pause and then he laughed. "I thought as much," he answered, his voice instantly sounding lighter and more energetic. "I hoped as much," he added almost breathless with barely suppressed excitement. "Have you had them processed yet?"

"No, I…"

"Thank heavens," he interrupted. "We must make sure no one else sees them."

"Well, just how do we go about doing that? I mean, it used to be a piece of cake—smelly, but easy. Now, I don't know how…"

"I have a friend," confided Horatio.

I laughed. I remembered Horatio's old gang of ex-spies. "Which nursing home is it this time," I asked.

I usually enjoyed my infrequent road trips with Horatio. His cushy, "all the bells and whistles" Bentley was such a stark contrast to my new little economy car. The elegance and comfort of the Bentley seemed to warrant whatever extra maintenance and expense was called for, especially since Horatio was the one footing the bill. But this time was different.

We drove to Nashville in silence—each afraid the photographs wouldn't come out. Too much, or too little light—a shaky hand—any number of mishaps—and Billy could well be shaking hands with "Old Sparky" on death row in Teddyville.

On the way back home, we were even more silent. Like Montgomery Gentry says, "Ya could'a heard a heart break."

I was depressed and deep in thought, wondering if I had made a huge mistake—sending us on a wild goose-chase and raising Horatio's hopes—for nothing. The flat, two-dimensional photographs were difficult to decipher. The marks I had seen so easily on Millicent's body had disappeared into shadows on the film—leaving only a few lines that could be anything.

And to make matters worse, Horatio had uncovered the sad and bitter secret his photographer friend in the Nashville nursing home was keeping from his buddies.

"He was in the trenches, you know—the foxholes, everywhere—jumping out of planes with the toughest airborne infantry—the 87th. He would willingly go to the ends of the Earth and do anything for that next big photograph. He was fearless."

"He still is, Horatio," I reminded quietly.

"I know."

We resumed our sad and uneasy silence. Terminal pancreatic cancer has that effect on a conversation.

"But we got the pictures," we both said after a moment, then laughed softly at our synchronicity.

"Wonder what they mean?"

"I only hope we can discover something useful," he sighed.

"He'll be all right, Horatio. He's still a tough old bird." I patted his gloved hand on the steering wheel. "Just like you."

CHAPTER SEVEN

Horatio cheered up the minute he saw my mother walking the dog down by the raspberry patch. She paused for a moment to free the hem of her skirt from a briar, and I heard him sigh again—this time with contentment.

"Did you ever see anything so lovely?" he sighed.

"Look. I'm the wrong person to answer that question. I still haven't gotten over her calling Leonard a rude and disgusting lout this morning. If you have any pull at all, Horatio, please make her let up on my meal ticket. Her constant carping is getting old."

"My dear, if I had any leverage at all, she'd have been Mrs. Horatio Raleigh ten years ago instead of just the last three glorious months." He turned and smiled before he eased out of the Bentley. "Looks like we'll both have to exercise more patience."

"Humph!" But I was smiling, and more than a little jealous. I sat in the car and watched the spring return to my old friend's step as he headed down to the berry patch. How I missed having someone in my own life who could heal my heart and salve my soul like that. And then I caught sight of Cassie peering up out of the brambles, hoisting a big bucket triumphantly over her head, and my own spirits lifted a notch or two. Nothing like a sweet daughter and a bowl of raspberry cobbler to correct a slight hitch in the universe.

Mother made the cobbler the old fashioned way—a simple, yet rich sheet of pastry layered with berries cooked in sugar until they bordered on bursting, then topped with heavy sweet whipped cream flavored with vanilla. This had been a day for silences and dessert was no exception. No one spoke until the last incredible bite had been consumed, and then we all spoke at once.

"My lord, that was good," declared Horatio. "Anna, dear, you have surpassed yourself."

"And what about me?" grinned Cassie. "Don't I get some credit? Brambles, briars, thorns—does that ring a bell?"

"The absolutely the best berries ever, Cass. I'll remember you next time I look in the mirror and watch my derriere spreading."

The evening was perfect. We took our coffee out to the patio where we sat under a blanket of sparkling heavenly lights, enjoying the peace and quiet at the end of a stressful day.

And then I had to go and ruin it.

"How's the diminutive Doc, Cassie? Has he walked under any good cows lately?"

"Oh! Mom! You're so…you're so infuriating!" And she stomped off to the house without another word.

"Damn."

"Well, what did you expect, dear?"

"It was just a joke. But he is really short. She can't deny that," I snorted indelicately. "And besides, they look silly together."

"So did Sonny and Sherry, and look how successful they were."

"Yeah, until they got a divorce, and he skied into a tree," I shot back, ignoring her gaffe.

The next morning I got up at the crack of dawn, anxious to take our photographs apart with my fancy software. I was chomping at the bit, but had promised Horatio on the way back from Nashville that I would wait for him to begin working.

Since his retirement, Horatio had forgotten the meaning of the phrase, "bright and early," so I convinced Mother, who was an early riser herself, to encourage that distinguished gentleman to have an early breakfast. She used the excuse of a surplus of Cassie's delicious hand-picked raspberries to tempt him, not realizing that the mere pleasure of her company was more than enough.

I helped her set the table on the back porch while we waited for him to shower and shave. I even dared the wet grass to pluck a few roses for the centerpiece. Just as I was putting the finishing touch on the flower arrangement, Cassie hurried out on her way to breakfast with her new boyfriend. She flashed me a perky little smile and took the wind out of my sails by referring to her date as *petite-dejeuner* before I had the chance.

I was contemplating the disastrous possibility of elfin grandchildren with British accents, an insatiable taste for treacle and a house full of budgies, when Horatio came out on the porch.

"What's bothering our lovely author this morning?" he crooned as he winked at my mother. "Could it be that her fickle little chick is showing more than the usual interest in our new veterinarian?"

"Yeah, all right," I answered sourly. "Now's your chance to make some smart comment about "all creatures great and small," then maybe we can eat." I flounced back to the kitchen, stumbling awkwardly on the trailing belt of my housecoat as I returned with the butter. "Rats!" I murmured. The morning wasn't turning out like I had expected at all.

And to make matters worse, Horatio appeared to be in no mood to abandon the breakfast table. After finishing his mammoth meal of shirred eggs, country ham, raspberries with cream, and home-made biscuits—he drank cup after cup of coffee and made calf eyes at an openly flirtatious Anna Howard Sterling until I thought I was going to scream.

Finally, after they had ignored my presence for a full forty-five minutes, I could endure no more. "Well," I quipped nastily. "I'm about as necessary as a pyramid roofer. I'll put this stuff away when you're done, Mother—or maybe just leave it out since it's so close to suppertime. Meanwhile, I'll throw on some jeans and get to work on those photographs." I cleared my throat loudly. "Is that okay with you, Horatio?"

"Right you are, Paisley, dear. Be there in a moment," he grinned. "Soon as Anna and I finish our coffee."

A nice hot shower went a long way to curing my bad mood, but once again the fates frowned when they gave me a "mommy dearest" moment with some wire coat hangers. Vowing to change dry cleaners, I shrugged into an overly starched cotton shirt and stiff jeans and made my way into the library. Horatio found me slapping down the billowing cotton front of my blouse when he joined me.

"Paisley, you never fail to provide an amusing moment," he observed with a chuckle.

"Delighted to be of service," I snapped. "At least I'm good for something."

"A mite piqued because Cassandra has shut you out of this romance of hers?"

"No! Well, yes," I amended. Then groaned, "She usually gives me some hint of what's going on. I never pry," I hastened to assure him, "but she always waxes poetic in the beginning. You know, "he's so wonderful—he hung the moon—blah, blah romantic crap, *ad nausium.*"

"But this time it's different."

"Yes," I moaned. "Do you think that means it's serious? I mean, I love the Queen and all, and you know how I feel about scones and Earl Grey, but the idea of Cassie marrying someone from another country and going there to live…"

"You did it," he reminded me bluntly.

"I know. That's why I'm so worried."

"And he's short."

"Oh, forget *short*! He could have four left feet for all I care, just so he wants to live in Rowan Springs."

Horatio sat down in the big leather chair in front of the fireplace where he was accustomed to warming his toes in the winter, and began the process of readying his pipe for a smoke.

"Do you mind, my dear?" he asked, holding it aloft.

"Umm," I grunted. He knew I loved the smell of his fancy imported tobacco.

"I've been observing this particular Romeo and Juliet with some interest," he confided. "And if it makes you feel any better, my conclusion is that your daughter has another agenda."

"But what?"

"That particular point has eluded me," he confessed. "Now where are those photographs?"

CHAPTER EIGHT

The clever little gizmos inside my fancy new computer worked their magic as we sat back and watched. Following the idiot-proof instructions on the screen, in no time at all the photographs I had taken against Horatio's wishes appeared.

We zoomed in and examined each and every angle with no results until it occurred to me to reverse the images so we could have a mirror view without the mirror.

"Nineteen and fifty-four!" we shouted in triumphant unison.

"What does that mean, Horatio?"

"Damned if I know," he whispered the unaccustomed profanity.

"And that does *so* look like initials!"

"I can't argue that with you now, my dear. And I'm truly sorry I didn't take you more seriously when we had a chance to call this matter to someone else's attention."

"Let that be a lesson," I teased. "Treat Paisley More Seriously 101."

"And lesson number two could be: uncover the face of the body when taking photographs so it can be identified."

"Oh, jeez, that's going to be a problem, isn't it?"

"'Fraid so, my dear. Even if those scars provide the evidence that could clear Billy Arlequin's name, we can't prove they belong to Millicent. These pictures could be of anyone, as far as the law is concerned. Only you and I know that it really is Madame Grazziani's corpse."

"Isn't that enough? Couldn't we testify to that? I have no problem swearing it was her. So can you."

"*I* can," he amended. "You had no business being there in the first place. Remember that little point if you want me to stay in business. A very lucrative business," he added under his breath.

"No," he decided, shaking his head, "you will have to stay in the background on this one, Paisley. And even so, I don't know how it will look when I offer up these photographs. Most people are very particular about the way they want their dearly departed treated. I would imagine that the possibility of a little postmortem slide show would be high on their list of irreverent behavior."

"What do you care? You're out of it, for the most part, that is."

He gave me a stern and reproachful look. "I'll give you the benefit of believing there was no disrespect intended in your remarks, but I'll also remind you that this is a family business. I love my nephew. I don't mind what happens to me, but I could never allow a blemish on the family name for his sake." He puffed thoughtfully on his pipe, his brow creased in a frown, as he decided, "No, we'll just have to think of another way to clear Billy."

Horatio's verdict signaled an end to his interest in my photographs of Millicent's abdomen. Out of respect for his company, I turned away from the computer and followed his desultory conversation for a few minutes until Mother, much to our combined relief, interrupted.

"I'm taking a little drive down to the lake," she announced gaily. "Anyone want to tag along? Paisley? Horatio?"

That sprightly gentleman was up and out the door before you could say, "Hey, I thought he was almost seventy!"

I waved energetically as they drove down the drive, then immediately turned back with renewed enthusiasm to my computer. Now that Horatio was gone, I could indulge in whatever fantasy I wished. The marks on Milly's tummy were game pieces on my own personal Scrabble board. As long as I didn't have a dissenting audience, they could spell out any word I cared to speculate upon.

I started with the area around the umbilicus where I remembered seeing an "m" or possibly a "w." And there they were again— barely visible as they edged up out of a fold in her wrinkled old skin. Unfortunately, both my hands had been occupied with the little disposable camera, and I hadn't been able to pull the flesh taut enough to reveal more. I cursed softly and then smiled, realizing that this was what I liked, a puzzle that was truly tough. Anything else would have been disappointing and lost my interest in a heartbeat.

I zoomed in closer and copied the image, then using the copy, I began to extend the lines and tweak the angles—hoping they would make sense. After several tries, I came up with at least two, maybe three, possibilities—all involving various combinations of "m's," and "n's," "w's" and the certainty of the number, "1954." Crossing my fingers, and assuming the number corresponded to a year, I decided that my next stop should be the archives of the George P. Whitherspoon Public Library.

Mother was right. It was a lovely almost fall day. For a brief moment, I entertained the possibility of heading down to the lake and tracking them down for an early supper at Fox Trot Charlie's Marina, but the memory of their simpering, lovey-dovey conversation at breakfast was enough to quell my appetite. Let them have their privacy, I decided. For all I knew, they might be doing more than conversing.

Cursing old love, as well as young love, and the lack of love in between for me, I climbed in my car and drove downtown.

The librarian was a pleasant young woman with pretty auburn hair and a brilliant smile. Trudy Shaw was one of those people who are lucky in their vocation. She truly loved books. I found her on her hands and knees energetically cleaning out the bottom shelves in the Reference Room.

"Need some help?"

"Hi, Paisley. Nope. I'm making room for a brand spankin' new set of encyclopedia. Isn't that wonderful?"

"How come?" I knew the library was always on the losing end of the city's budget cuts. Their so-called Reference Room had been a joke for years.

"Millicent Grazzini!" she declared, her face beaming. "She left us enough money for six new computer stations, too. Isn't that wonderful? And just to think, the last time she was in here I yelled at her for tearing out pages from one of the new magazines. The dear old thing!" Trudy sat back on her heels, and dusted off her sleeves as she sighed, "I feel really guilty about it now. I had no idea she loved the written word as much as I do."

"You should see her stomach."

"What's that, Paisley?"

"Er, nothing. Trudy, I need to get to the archives.

"You know where the keys are. Have at it. Just follow the drill and put everything back where you got it."

I left her to cleaning and made my way to the older wing of the building. When I was a little girl, this was the entire library: ten stacks of very old, and very moldy books—all donated by folks who no longer wanted them. There had been no "library fund" and everything had been bought with support from the various women's clubs who kept a very close watch on what was allowed on those hallowed shelves. It had been my first experience with censorship. I remembered with amusement my outrage at not being able to find certain authors' works in the library because they were "tacky Yankees with dirty mouths."

It was at least ten degrees cooler in the basement—and musty. As I pushed aside stacks of journals and old ledgers, dust motes floated up in the air like sleepy fairies awakened from a long nap and my nose began to twitch and tickle.

My goal was over against the outside wall—three ancient metal cabinets whose creaky drawers held the microfiche files of old newspapers; but getting there wasn't easy. Trudy hadn't been as diligent with her cleaning down here in the archives. There were stacks of boxes and cartons on the floor, and I cursed and stumbled in the gloom as I picked my way through the mess.

I found what I wanted after several tries, but the cabinets were old and full to the brim. The weight of the drawers made pulling them out difficult and getting them back in place was well nigh impossible. I was glad no one could hear me because my curses took on a very colorful note when I broke a nail and skinned a knuckle.

Finally, I took my hard earned prize—a stack of microfiche at least a foot high—back to one of the old wooden tables. I blew the dust off one side and set them down carefully in what I hoped was the correct order. Of course, the entire exercise was ruined as I tugged the plastic cover off the reader and knocked the whole stack of files off on the floor in the process.

By the time I had picked everything up, cleaned off a chair, turned on the machine, and waited for it to warm up, I was worn out and ready to go home. My hands were filthy, I was sweating profusely, and my nose itched like crazy. I rubbed it carefully against my shoulder, trying to avoid getting my face as dirty as the rest of me, but finally had to give in and scratch.

The dust I had stirred up began to settle—mostly in my throat—and I coughed and sneezed while the old reading machine hemmed and hawed into life. I chuckled, thinking we sounded like twins in our noisy discomfort. The machine sounded even worse than I did, and when the little green ready light blinked on I was somewhat surprised that the ancient thing still worked.

Since I had no idea what I was looking for, my research soon took on an air of resigned desperation. For an hour or two, I poured over the old newspaper pages, working the slide lever back and forth, up and down; hoping something in the dizzying display would catch my eye. The stack of film descended rapidly, and I was halfway through it when the headache began.

I had managed to ignore the scratchy throat and the stuffed up nose—the dirt and dust, and the certainty of more insects than just the errant silverfish I had seen scurrying into the corner, but the pounding between my eyes was too painful to dismiss. I turned away from the machine, lay my head down, and closed my eyes.

After a moment or two the pain and the dizziness receded, but I remained where I was—too tired and bored to resume my task.

The faint sounds of life in Rowan Springs seeped through the cracks in the old windows high above me. Long ago someone had painted over the glass to keep curious passersby from peering into the dusty recesses of the library, and only a faint glow from what was a bright sunny day outside came through.

I heard a car horn in the distance, a child's shrill and angry cry, and then the carillon from the Presbyterian Church spire as it pealed out the half hour. Two women laughed as they walked past the library, their high heels clicking smartly on the sidewalk, and then silence as I nodded off.

I awoke hours, or minutes later—I had no idea how much time had elapsed. It was too dark to read my watch. The light on the other side of the windows was considerably dimmer and the bulb on the microfiche machine had burned out. As if that wasn't bad enough, I had no idea where the switch for overhead light was.

I stood up, creaking and cracking joints and muscles still sore from my tennis match with Mother, and stumbled around looking for the light switch. As the room grew darker, I decided to abandon my search and find the way out before it was too late to see anything.

I had gotten turned around when I first came down the stairs and it took me a minute or two to find them again. I was hungry now as well as tired, and the old wooden steps seemed even steeper. I was more than ready for a nice warm bath and a patio session complete with soft music, a plate of Mother's goodies, and a chilled glass of Australian.

I pulled and tugged, but it was no use. The damned door was locked, and I was trapped in the dark in the ancient basement of the George P. Whitherspoon Public Library.

CHAPTER NINE

I struggled with the old-fashioned brass knob, but it wouldn't budge. I was trapped with no light, no food or water, and nothing but my cell phone to help me out of my dilemma.

I called the library desk, but there was no answer. Unfortunately, I had to call Mother.

When she finally stopped laughing, she promised to call Trudy at home and get someone to liberate me. I sat down on the top step to wait.

And I waited, and I waited.

I tried to call her back, but the number was busy. Mother had an aversion to the "call waiting" feature on our telephone. She has always thought it unfriendly to say the least and unmannerly at the worst. Right about now she was probably calling all her little old lady friends to tell them about her zany daughter and had no intention of interrupting one second of her important conversation.

I waited.

I was just about to nod off again when I heard a key turn in the lock and the creak of the old door as it opened. I fell backwards onto the floor of the library and looked up into the laughing face of Andy Joiner, Rowan Springs' own stalwart Chief of Police.

"Well, well, well," he said. "Seems like our little mystery writer wrote herself into a corner. Now just how did you go and do that?"

"Trudy went off and left me, that's how," I growled.

"Oh, yeah, that. Your mother called me when she couldn't reach her. I called her assistant, and she told me one of Trudy's kids had a problem at school. Nothing serious, but she had to leave early. Guess she did forget you after all."

He reached down and helped me up with one effortless pull of his strong right arm. I bounded to my feet, swaying for a moment, and leaned against the doorframe while my head stopping swimming.

"Dizzy?" he asked, his face betraying a sincere concern.

"Thirty-year old microfiche reader for four hours, and maybe a little starvation," I said.

"I was just about to head out to the DQ. Wanna join me?"

"I'd love to, but I made this promise to Cassie last year—fats and carbs and stuff like that are forbidden fruit." I felt no need to add that I had fallen from grace only a few days ago since, so far, no one had found me out.

"They have a new menu now. The wife loves their grilled chicken salad. Maybe you could…?

The grumbling in my stomach responded loudly. "Lead on, MacDuff!" I agreed.

Andy decided we should go in his cruiser then he would bring me back to my car after we ate. Being my mother's daughter, I couldn't help but wonder how it might look to someone else.

"Where's Connie? Doesn't she mind your taking beautiful unattached females out to dine without her?"

"She would, if I did," he teased. "She's over at the school helping with some kind of banquet—something about planning for the new academic year."

"I thought all your little ones were big ones now."

"Flora's a senior this year. Then we'll be done. She's got a scholarship for four years at Georgetown—if she can keep her grades up."

"Good grief, Andy! I had no idea. That's wonderful."

"Don't look at me," he chuckled. "Connie's the one with all the smarts. All's I got are those GOB genes."

"GOB?"

"Good ole boy."

"Yeah, right! You're just a poor dumb schmuck with hayseed for brains, a daughter with a 4.0, and a wife who still looks like Miss America. Poor you."

"Let's just say I've been lucky."

"You really have, Andy," I agreed, all my teasing over and done with. "Too bad Billy Arlequin wasn't so lucky."

"Paisley," he warned, his voice slipping into a low growl.

"I mean, poor guy, with Madame Grazziani just up and kicking like that. Must have been such a shock. And then being arrested for her murder…bummer."

The windows were down and Andy drove slowly, letting the night air cool us as we skirted the perimeter of his domain—the fiefdom he had been appointed to guard. He ignored my needling query, his face set and confident—the king of the jungle avoiding the persistent buzz of a pesky mosquito.

We ate in silence. The salad was good but the constant parade of trays overflowing with hot fries and chili-dogs filing past our booth made my mouth water. It wasn't long before my unhealthy desire for junk food reared its ugly head. My pique at not being able to weasel any information about Millicent's death from Andy was overpowered by the intense desire to make an absolute pig of myself. I decided to try and make him an accessory before the fact.

"Wanna share some fries?"

Andy shook his big head, his shaggy hair falling into his eyes— bringing out that boyish look that made those who didn't know him underestimate his acumen.

"Promised Connie," he mumbled over a mouthful of grilled chicken.

"You're just a freaking tower of strength, aren't you?" I snapped.

He put his fork down and folded his beefy arms over each other on the table. "What's up, Paisley? You're as skittish as a colt. And that's twice you've bad-mouthed me today."

"Sorry." I stopped myself from biting my lower lip just in time to keep from looking like a kid with a hand in the cookie jar.

"Is it because I teased you about your looks? 'Cause if it is, I can assure you I was just jokin,' but you know that. Besides, talk about what Connie wouldn't like—praising another woman's good looks is right there on the top of the list."

I grinned in spite of myself. I hated to admit it, but that comment had been one source of my irritation.

"So I'm gorgeous, eh?"

He blushed and picked up his fork again to attack the remaining lettuce on his plate. "That's what the boys on the force say."

"Wow! A group compliment."

"Of course, they also think you're nosey and impetuous and generally a big fat pain in the ass. And to a man they wish you'd mind your own business and stay out of theirs." He finished off his dinner and downed half of his biggie ice tea in one swallow. When he set the cup down he held the lemon slice between his front teeth like a big yellow smile.

"You're so *high school*, Andy Joiner," I responded heatedly. "You know, I'm not just your average citizen. There were more than a few times in the past couple of years when you welcomed my expert help."

"I know there've been more than a few times in the past when I've had to pull your bacon out of the fire, but *you* help *me*? When did that happen?"

"Oh, rats. You'll never admit it, so why bother."

He chuckled again, and then grew serious once more. "Paisley, this is one time when you'd better stay out of the fray. I will only say this once: there's more to this case than meets the eye, and it could prove very dangerous. Please believe me and drop whatever interest you have in Billy Arlequin."

Nobody was home when I got back to the farm. We used to laugh about the fact that the big old house never looked lonely or empty—too many ghosts, we said. But old houses cast long shadows and Mother had placed little gizmos in her lamps that turned them on at a certain time every night to create the illusion of life going on inside. She needn't have bothered. The house on Meadowdale Farm had a life of its own—like a forest where the sound of a falling tree could be heard even if no one was there to hear it. It didn't need people to be inhabited.

A big fat full moon hung like a tub of butter just over the horizon, and when I turned off the engine I could hear the tiny frogs singing in the little pond in back of the carriage house. An occasional "belly deep" from a much bigger bullfrog boomed out of the darkness in the reeds, and several cicadas added a brief staccato chorus.

I climbed up on the hood of the car and lay back against the warmth of the metal listening to the sounds of the night. A hint of honeysuckle from the back fence scented the light breeze and brought back memories of other nights like this in my childhood when the dinner dishes were washed and put away and there was nothing to do until bedtime but relax on the big back porch and talk about the events of the day.

Back then—at least for us—there was no need for a sleeping pill, or late night television as a cure for insomnia. The grownups worked too hard to feel the need of sleeping draughts, and we had not yet succumbed to the stupefying lure of the magic box. It was a time when children learned by listening to the hum of adult voices instead of being encouraged electronically by a brightly colored felt puppet to count or read.

After a scorching day the gathering mist would have covered the fields with a soft blanket of swirling greys and the cool breeze acted as both soporific and truth serum. As I perched on the edge of my little red chair I found out my grandfather was a die-hard Democrat while my father always voted for a Republican. From the two of them I learned how to agreeably disagree, but I also learned to step in like my gentle grandmother when voices got just a tad edgy. I learned a lot in those happy times, mostly how to love and be loved—how to treat my neighbors, and when to stand up for my rights.

I missed those wonderful evenings, but I was getting cold. The dew had fallen and the hood of the car had gradually lost its heat. High time, I decided, to stop reminiscing and go inside. I slid off into the gravel of the driveway—the noise made by my feet immediately calling a halt to the symphony of amorous amphibians— and headed toward the big old house and all of its beloved ghosts.

CHAPTER TEN

I trudged up the driveway, my moccasins scuffing up loose gravel like a little kid, stopping once when a piece of rock lodged in the toe of my shoe—that's when I heard the voices.

Startled, I stood absolutely still—waiting until I heard them again. One was Cassie, that much I could tell, but the other voice had a different rhythm—a strange cadence that was unfamiliar—and angry.

I crept closer, careful now not to make any more noise—straining to hear the conversation. Normally I tried to stay out of my daughter's business, but my protective motherly instincts took precedence over manners any day. Besides, it sounded like she might be in trouble.

"You must admit you've led me on a wee bit, lass."

"Absolutely not. I told you that I thought you were nice, that's all. And I'm beginning to change my opinion about that!"

"Look, dolly, I know when a lassie sets her cap for someone, and you gave out all the right signals. 'Tis not my imagination alone that tells me you want it as much as I do. Now come here and give us a kiss."

I started forward, then halted when I heard a resounding slap—a grunt, and the sound of someone's backside tumbling down the front steps. I raced around the corner of the house and came up short when I saw Cassie's date dusting off the seat of his trousers. He was headed resolutely back up the steps when I opened my mouth.

"Good evening."

The man stopped and turned around quickly, giving Cassie time to duck into the house and lock the screen door. It was protection—even if it was flimsy, but I had an idea that it would be more than enough with me on the scene. I couldn't tell for sure in the moonlight, but I would have bet that her date was beet red with anger and embarrassment.

"Uh, good evening, Mrs. DeLeon," he offered in a breathless voice. "I was just, um, saying good night to your lovely daughter. I'll be off now. Ta."

And he was gone—practically running to the car he had left down by the entrance. I stared after him a moment—shooting daggers with my eyes.

"Cassie? Are you all right?"

"You know perfectly well I'm just fine," she huffed. "You were out there in the dark snooping on me long enough."

"You sounded distressed. I was just concerned, that's all"

"You're nosey as a mother hen! You know perfectly well I can handle myself with any man." She unlocked the door for me and flounced off down the hallway toward the kitchen.

I followed.

She threw her purse on the counter and turned on me.

"*Now* what do you want?"

"I'm hungry," I complained. "All I had for supper was some stupid salad at…well, I'm still hungry."

She leaned closer and took a suspicious sniff of my clothes.

"You ate at the Dairy Queen, didn't you? And don't even try to deny it. You smell like a vat of salty lard."

"A salad, Cassie, I swear that's all I had. Andy Joiner can vouchsafe for me. He had one, too. Are you sure you're all right? You look a little flushed."

"Well, why wouldn't I be? No matter how hard I've tried, I still have a mother who cares more about a bacon double cheeseburger than she does her cholesterol count."

"Cassie," I chided gently, "this isn't about my cholesterol count and you know it."

She plopped down in a kitchen chair and burst into tears. "That filthy little pig," she wailed. "He tried to…he was going to…"

"Never mind, baby."

"Baby! That's all you think of me, and I'm *not* a baby. I could have handled it, you know. I'm just so…so…so damn mad."

"Oops, you're beginning to sound like your dear old mama," I chuckled and tried to put my arms around her but she shrugged me off.

"He was right, of course. I was leading him on, but it was all in a good cause." She looked up at me, her eyes shining brightly through the tears. "He had every reason to try and, well, you know; but I can't feel sorry for him, not after what I think I found out."

I knew better than to force any further attempts at maternal comfort on my offspring. Cassie had a fright, and she was angry with herself as well as her erstwhile date. Knowing that she had to go through the litany of how interfering I was, and how she could have taken care of everything by herself, I decided to wait until the fireworks were over for another try at a hug.

I reached back inside the refrigerator in a mighty effort to snare the half banana I'd left after breakfast without removing the milk, eggs, and orange juice that stood in my way.

Behind me in the kitchen Cassie blew her nose loudly and sniffed, "He's a drug dealer, you know—big time," she confided.

I straightened up quickly—but not in time to avoid the calamity that followed. The milk, eggs, orange juice, and a host of other cold, wet things tumbled out onto my feet and the kitchen floor bursting into a dazzling array of yuck. "Drug dealer? You're kidding?"

"Look what you've done," she accused. "And Gran's coming home any minute."

"Forget about Gran. What the hell did you *mean*, drug dealer?"

"I think it's pretty self-explanatory, don't you? Drug dealer, as in one who deals in drugs? Got it? Now get out of the way and let me clean up this mess while you go and change into something without food on it."

Aggie was asleep on my pillow as usual and gave me only a cursory glance when I entered the room. I tossed my discarded shirt so that it landed on her face, and grinned smugly when that provoked a low and very menacing growl.

"You stupid dog. Where were you a moment ago when your mistress was in peril?" She got up and shook herself violently, spreading little doggie hairs and other canine flotsam over my clean sheets, then walked daintily over to my other pillow and took up residence. She raised her left leg and licked her stomach deliberately, daring me to swat her one. I would have, too. Or at least I would have tried, but Cassie's bombshell was still ringing in my ears. I had to hurry if I wanted to wheedle the rest of the story out of her before Mother and Horatio came home.

Cassie had a glass of sweet tea and a bowl of fruit salad waiting for me when I returned. Knowing that I had to appease her, I sat down at the kitchen table and took a couple of bites of pineapple before I posed the burning question.

"So, you were saying that the good Dr. Haverstock is a drug dealer?"

"I said I *think* he's dealing in drugs," she said, making the point with her fork. "I noticed it the first time when I took Aggie in to have her teeth cleaned."

"I'd have to be on drugs myself to accomplish that little feat," I mumbled.

"Mom, if you're not going to be serious about this, then I'll go to bed and you can just forget about it."

"Sorry, honey. You were saying?"

"For one thing, Huntley's been through at least three assistants since he took over for Doc White."

"What's so strange about that? Mother can't even find someone to clean the gutters."

"And," she went on after casting a warning glance my way, "while I was in the waiting room I noticed some rather strange looking people coming in to pick up packages, and none of them had an animal with them. People generally take their dog or cat to the vet even if they're only picking up a prescription, or kibble, or a new leash. Kind of like they're showing it off."

"What did the packages look like? Big? Little?"

"Always small—little brown paper sacks, mostly. Like the ones you take your school lunch in if you don't have a lunch box."

I finished off my fruit salad and snagged an extra grape from her bowl.

"Huntley seemed nice—at first, anyway, and then he got sort of—well, I guess "coarse" is the right word for it." She slapped my hand away when I tried to steal another grape. "Yes," she said, considering, "he got coarse, and kind of naughty."

"Damn it, Cassie. What did he try to do?"

"Nothing overt really, that is not until tonight. He just started making innuendoes—things that tickled him to death but made me feel sort of slimy. I don't think he's really a very nice man, Mom."

"How could you have let yourself put up with that, Cassie? Things could have turned out much worse."

"I told you. I had good reason…"

"Good reason, my hind foot," I exploded. "You're not Leonard Paisley, or anything like him. You have no business playing detective."

"Neither do you, and you do it all the time!"

"That's different. I'm your mother, and I'm a grownup."

"Oh, yeah? And I'm not?"

We were both shouting now, and Aggie came scampering in to see what was going on. Remembering my gentle grandmother, I lowered my voice and tried to smooth things over, but I had already made a fatal mistake and, like a dummy, I proceeded to compound it.

"Of course, you are, sweetie, but I'm just a little more grownup than you are."

"Hah!"

"And you *are* relatively innocent."

She raised one eyebrow and smirked, "Do go on," she urged. "This should be fun."

"Well," I began, casting around desperately in my mind for something to say. "You lived in San Romero a long time. You were sheltered there. Of course, that was my fault, and your father's, and your grandparent's…"

"Mom…" she warned.

"You don't know much about stuff…bad stuff…and things." It sounded lame even to me so I switched horses in mid-stream. "And I don't even think Huntley Haverstock is a Brit. I mean, pulease—*lassie*? Who really says that?"

"John Connery, that's who," she countered.

"It's Sean Connery, and he's a Scot and you just proved my point, Cass. You really don't know all that much."

"So I'm stupid?" She jumped up from the table and stomped her foot on the kitchen floor. Alarmed, Aggie turned and ran back down the hallway—fluffy white tail flying at half-mast.

"That's what you're really getting at, isn't it? And why am I stupid? Because I don't know the names of a bunch of silly old movie stars? How smart is that, I ask you?'"

"Not stupid, sweetheart, just uninformed and maybe a little in-experienced."

"Only a little inexperienced?" she sneered.

"Okay—a lot."

"Well, that's just wonderful. Here I am trying to help you out by bringing you a real live mystery on a silver platter—a mystery right here in Rowan Springs. And you ungrateful…you…you…"

She picked up a grape and threw it at me as she ran out of the kitchen.

CHAPTER ELEVEN

Mother and Horatio found me sitting at the kitchen table, chin in hand, musing on the great joke the universe had played by making me a parent. When prompted, I declined to share that damning bit of information because, for one thing, the argument was between Cassie and me, and for another, I was too upset to discuss it front of Mother because I knew she would take Cassie's side just to get my goat. Instead, I went for the shock value of Cassie's startling claim.

"A drug dealer? That ordinary little man? I think not, dear. And certainly not doing business out of the animal hospital. That would be, well, almost obscene."

Horatio smiled gently, but wisely refused to comment. I, on the other hand jumped in without thinking—as usual.

"Don't be silly, Mother," echoing, I was quite sure, Horatio's unspoken thoughts.

"What do you mean, dear?" she asked too sweetly.

"An animal clinic has the same access to drugs as a regular clinic—more, probably."

"That's not what I mean, and you know it," she snapped.

I took one look at her—cheeks flushed, head held high, dainty feet slightly parted, all primed and ready for me to fire one—and for the second time that night I remembered my grandmother's gentle ways.

"I'm sleepy," I yawned and rose. "'Night, Horatio, 'night, Mother."

"Humm."

I paused outside of Cassie's door, listening for a moment, afraid to knock—afraid of making things worse. Better to sleep on it, I decided. I had already done enough damage for today—and it wasn't even midnight.

The price of an argument with Cassie was always the loss of a good night's sleep. I decided not to even try fooling myself by getting into bed and instead made my way to library. It was a great night for an early fire—cool, crisp and chill—with a definite hint of persimmon in the air. School had started early in August this year—the result of snow days to make up—and I knew there was a football game tonight. I considered briefly sneaking out to attend, but it was no fun sneaking out when you were an adult and already had all the permission needed.

I fiddled with the CD player for a moment and came up with some wonderfully romantic boleros. I turned the volume up "loud enough to command attention yet not loud enough to disturb anyone else," turned off the lights, and curled up on the big red chintz sofa to enjoy my sulk in solitude.

Despite my efforts to the contrary, my thoughts kept going back to Cassie's assertion that Huntley Haverstock was a drug dealer. I found that idea very unsettling. I liked my puzzles to come one at a time so I could enjoy each one to the fullest. Millicent's auto-engraved body was my conundrum *du jour*, and I wasn't ready to have my attention divided.

But I had to admit that Cassie, bless her heart, had the right idea. I did need some new story material, and I had promised Horatio not to expose Millicent's terrible little secret. Maybe the vet wasn't really a drug dealer, but I thought it entirely possible that he had something to hide or he wouldn't have run off with his tail between his legs when I popped up unexpectedly.

For one thing, Haverstock was so stereotypically English that he was almost a caricature. His "lassie" this, and "ta" that, came right out of the dialogue of a mediocre Rank film from the thirties. And even if he were truly British, I had a hard time believing everything about Huntley Haverstock was for real. For one thing, my memory kept tap dancing around his name. I was certain I'd heard it somewhere before—the same name with a different face hovering at the edges of my mind.

I had to marvel, though, at Cassie's cheeky decision to date him in an attempt to discover more fodder for my own personal literary mill. After some amount of cogitation I finally decided that no matter what she said, she probably didn't start out seeing him with that in mind, and only began to notice Huntley's supposed hanky-panky when she began to tire of his charms. Too bad, I thought, that Aggie couldn't speak—she would make a great little spy, because I knew I wouldn't get another word out of her angry mistress. If Huntley Haverstock was up to mischief, then mischief had won.

I fell asleep on that thought, dreaming of endless tea parties where Mother poured, as Cassie, dressed to the nines in a frilly dress and frou-frou hat, flitted from table to table sampling iced teacakes and jam scones. Aggie was there, too—trying to tell me something just like Lassie in those old three handkerchief movies where the dog limps and plays dead and generally wrecks a little kid's mental state for days.

I woke up in a quandary, wondering what the stupid dog could possible know that I did not.

In spite of the night spent away from my bed, I felt rested and ready to face the day and all the daughters in it. What I hadn't counted on was the mother.

"Paisley, I need you to drive me around town."

"And a hearty good morning to you, too, Mother dear."

"And don't be sassy, my girl, or I can promise you it will be a very long day indeed."

After hours of waiting in her car while she delivered homemade soup and corn muffins to those friends of hers from Sunday School who were ailing—and forbidden to change the dial on her car radio from that mindlessly bland, so-called "classical" music that made you wish devoutly for electric shock therapy—I came up with one of what Cassie called my 'hare-brained schemes.'

Suddenly restless and eager to be on my quest, I turned around and counted the remaining soup containers and muffins still to be delivered. By rapidly devouring four muffins and pouring a container of soup in the midst of some really lovely pansies in front of Mary Beth Tatum's house, I managed to shorten the house calls by one and was happily heading home with Mother a mere thirty minutes later.

"I could have sworn I had another container of soup. And I really thought I had enough muffins left to take some to Horatio's nephew. He's batching it this week, poor dear, and he adores homemade bread. Too bad his fiancée doesn't like to… Paisley, are you sure something didn't fall out of the car?"

"For the fifth time—no, Mother," I lied. "I was very careful." Although, truth be told, it didn't fall out. And I was very careful. I didn't spill a drop when I poured the soup out and hid the plastic container in the flowerbed.

By the time we pulled up the long circular drive of Meadowdale Farm I was feeling somewhat of ashamed of my behavior. After all, Mother was just being the good soul that she was: a kind-hearted southern lady looking out for those who were ill or infirmed. Was I so uncharitable and mean-spirited that I couldn't give up one morning to help Lady Bountiful?

The answer was simple. I was mean, *and* uncharitable—especially when I was bored to tears and subjected to three hours of mindless musical Pablum pretending to be culture. And besides, I most desperately wanted to be on my way.

I helped Mother carry in the boxes that had protected her precious leather seats from errant muffin crumbs and accidental soup drips, and went in search of Aggie. After all, she was a major player in my little scheme.

"Good doggie," I crooned as I attempted to mold my face into what might pass for a genuine "I really do like you" grin.

She raised her suspicious head from the nest of down in my favorite pillow and ever so carefully lifted one side of her little black doggie lips in a snarl that contained worlds of contempt. She was so insolent that I didn't feel the least bit dishonest when I asked the magic question.

"Wanna go?"

The dog was up and off the bed in two seconds flat. She pawed impatiently at the back door while I explained to Mother that I would be back in an hour and was taking the dog out for some air and maybe a doggie cone at the DQ.

"But Paisley, you *never*…"

And we were gone in a flash.

* * * *

Beside herself with canine joy, Aggie stuck her fuzzy little head out the window and let the wind blow her long beard and eyebrows back from her face in a furry white ruff that made her look almost…well, cute. Not cute enough, however, to make me regret making her part and parcel of my nefarious plan to infiltrate enemy territory using her as my Trojan horse, er, dog.

CHAPTER TWELVE

From some of Horatio's wry comments, I had gathered that our own local vet had taken advantage of Huntley's sudden appearance by going on a long over-due vacation with his wife and children. After giving him a cursory tour of the clinic, Dr. Quentin White had waved goodbye to a bemused Huntley Haverstock and jumped into his twelve year-old farm truck to race home and pick up Sally Mae and the kids for a flight to Florida's golden beaches.

Even a seasoned professional would have had a hard time picking up from that point, especially with the differences in language and treatment protocols, but if Huntley were a fake in the medicine department as well as in the Brit department, like I thought, then he had fooled more people than Cassie. His borrowed waiting room was full of patients—large and small, furry, feathered and scaly, and all of them were squawking, bleating or barking at once.

I tried to remember where I had seen the receptionist before while I waited my turn at her desk. When I mentally painted her stringy grey hair brown, and dressed her in jeans and a checkered shirt instead of a wrinkled white uniform, it came to me.

Worrying on a hangnail and chewing on a number two pencil, Tillie Dunn barely paused to look up as I approached her desk.

"How's the pony?"

"Huh? What?"

"That wonderful pony you rode in the Bright Leaf Festival parade a couple of years ago."

Tillie beamed up at me.

"You saw me and Gaucho?"

"Sure did," I grinned, and this time it was genuine. Tillie and the pony had put on a pretty nifty show. I had been impressed.

"Gaucho, well," she sighed, "both of us are a little too old for showing off now, but we sure did have fun for awhile." She paused and attacked the hangnail again. "You're Cassie's mom, right? Can I help you with something?"

I had decided on the way over to use the same chief complaint for Aggie that Cassie had so rudely urged on her grandmother last year when we were faking our way into another doctor's office. It's only fair, I thought, and it serves her right.

Tillie didn't believe me.

"Are you sure she has worms. I mean, she's here all the time with Cassie since Dr. Haverstock took over. I would have thought…"

The flush that rose up from her neck to her cheekbones made her look years younger and much healthier than someone who reportedly smoked five packs a day and only ate bologna sandwiches and number two pencils.

I tried unsuccessfully to control my smirk by pressing my lips together and pulling them to the side. I'm sure it made me look like I had a twitch and a booger. Finally, I let go and grinned broadly. Tillie grinned back and we shared a private moment until she remembered she was over-worked and underpaid. She blew a wisp of hair back from her eyes and vowed tersely that she'd work me in as soon as she possible.

"Your doggie won't need a full physical since she's been here, er…well, you know. We probably can just get a stool sample and let you go. I can call in some medicine to the pharmacy if she needs it. You won't even have to see the doctor."

Yanking hard on Aggie's tail with one hand, I poked none too gently at a tiny freckled spot on her little pink tummy with the other.

"Did I tell you she's been crying out like that when we touch her here?"

Predictably, the dog snarled and snapped viciously at my finger, but for once I was prepared. Her teeth coming together without my pinky in the middle made a sound a crocodile would have been proud of and caused heads to turn as the other waiting clients cradled their precious pets protectively in their arms.

"Fine," snapped Tillie, her good humor and patience at an end. "But it'll be an hour, maybe more. Take a seat."

During the two hours that followed, I got acquainted with more people and their pets than I wanted to know in a lifetime. After the first ten minutes passed and Aggie saw that we were going nowhere, she scratched around until she found a comfortable spot on my lap, then settled down to resume her mid-day nap. Much to my sorrow, people suddenly felt safer approaching me to show off their own beloved animals. After I had properly admired a croupy parakeet, an asthmatic schnauzer, and a lovely but skittish Siamese, I found myself cornered by a short, fat little woman who claimed to be in Mother's Sunday school class and was the proud owner what had to be one of the world's fattest felines.

"He's almost nineteen now, but as spry as ever. Can't hold his wee-wee though, so we can't take trips—well, except to here, and to my mother's." The woman leaned in closer just in case any of the other people waiting gave a damn. "Mother's blind, you know, and she's lost her sense of smell so…well, I'm used to it, but some people, my uppity *sister* for one, says cat urine…" She proudly held almost thirty pounds of incontinent cat up by the armpits allowing the rest of him to spill back over her lap like a furry puddle of liquid mercury.

"…but it's a small price to pay for wuvin' my wootsie dootsie. Isn't it my precious kitty? Ohhh, wookee dat pretty face on my wittle baby boy, isn't he adorable?"

I tried in vain to pretend an admiration for the offending puss without taking a breath, but the pervasive odor of obese cat in need of a diaper was too much. I coughed, then gagged, then retched, praying fervently all the while that I would not lose my breakfast on Woosie Dootsie.

"Well!"

And suddenly, I was thankfully alone on my end of the waiting room. I squirmed carefully in the little plastic bucket seat trying to find a more comfortable position without waking up Beowulf in drag, but the plastic was hard and my backside was a trifle wider than it had been a month or so ago.

By the time Tillie called my name, my right butt cheek was completely without sensation. It was this condition that caused me to walk with a queer sort of lurching motion as I made my way back to the examining room. Aggie slept on in my arms until the scent of other frightened and distressed animals reached her delicate little black nose. She opened one sleepy brown eye, looked up to see me instead of her beloved Cassie, and retaliated by biting me as hard as she could.

"Damn dog!"

I practically threw her on the stainless steel top of the examining table. Her sharp nails clicked a frantic tattoo on the metal surface as she tried to get away from big bad me and maintain her balance at the same time. When I saw that she was intent on escaping, I made a grab for her tail and came away with handful of feathery white plumes as she leapt from the end of the table and took off.

"Damnation!"

I ran after her—and from a window at the end of the hall caught a passing glimpse of Huntley Haverstock as he backed rapidly out of the driveway in a brand new Land Rover.

"Damn again and again!" I shouted.

I popped my head in and out of examining rooms like a Jack-in-the-box until I finally found the dog cornered in a room at the end of the building—apparently in the area of the clinic that served as a laboratory. A long shelf on one wall held an array of microscopes. Other shelves held beakers, Petrie dishes and vials filled with noxious looking solutions.

Aggie stood her ground—growling and pretending to be six feet tall and twice as wide. I had to admire the little twit. She almost had me fooled, but I had learned over the years that if you ignored her in circumstances like these she would soon drop her fearsome stance and forget what she was about.

I had already forgotten.

My attention was focused on a rough wooden table in the middle of the room where a collection of little brown paper sandwich bags sat on blatant display. Cassie hadn't been making that part of her story up! Without even thinking about it, I grabbed two of the little bags and hastily stuffed them in my leather tote. Maybe I wouldn't get to confront the good doctor, but I had some first class evidence and that was enough for me.

I whistled for Aggie and almost fell over with surprise when she obediently trotted after me down the hall and out the clinic door with the wisps of what had been her once glorious tail wagging proudly behind her.

Without a word to anyone, I hastily opened the car door and boosted the Aggie up and in with the well-placed toe of my moccasin.

"Mission accomplished, dog!"

She didn't understand that we were celebrating until I pulled in at the DQ and got her a doggie dish to go. We were the best of pals all the way home.

CHAPTER THIRTEEN

"It's manure."

"No, it can't be!"

"Look, Cassie, the paper bags even have the location of where the specimen was found written on them. Look, this one says, 'Rowan Springs, Farm 239, Lot 2, Area 21.'"

"It's got to be some kind of contraband, Mom. I just know it is."

"Good old fashioned cow dung, nothing more, nothing less. And a great deal smellier than some I've encountered."

"Then, that's it! Some kind of chemical agent designed to camouflage the odor of drugs—to keep the dogs from sniffing it in airports and stuff."

"Cassie," I began patiently, "if it looks like a duck and quacks like a duck…

Cassie sank down in a kitchen chair, her mouth drawn down in a pout that would work on anyone but a mother who had long ago gotten used to it. But all things considered, I was too happy to be back in her good graces to argue any more.

"Oh, what the hell. It works for me. Call the DEA."

"Mom, don't be silly. It's just that I *so* wanted it to be a juicy little tidbit for one of Leonard's lurid stories—you know, to do my bit and all."

I smiled at my lovely offspring. "Cassie," I responded softly, "You've way more than done your bit over the years by growing up to be the sort of daughter I never dreamed I could have. Imagine me, the black sheep of the Sterling family, having a pearl like you?"

She snuffled and grinned at me. "You mixed your metaphors. Besides, you're not the black sheep and you know it."

"I may not have been when I was younger. I'm sure Mother and Dad were thrilled when I had the good sense to marry a bright young diplomat with a wonderful future. And they loved visiting us at the hacienda in San Romero. Who wouldn't have? It was a tropical paradise. But when I misplaced your Daddy and things started getting really bad, I lost some of my standing in their eyes by heading for New York and Pam instead of coming back home with my tail between my legs."

"Grandad understood, I know he did," soothed Cassie.

"Maybe, but Mother thought I should have put you first and come home for your sake. Leave you with her, if necessary, and go to New York on my own. She's never really forgiven me."

Cassie scooted closer and put her arms around me for a good hug.

"I'm so glad you didn't, Mom. I love Gran, and all, but I wouldn't have liked being left behind—not even one little bit."

I hugged her back and swiped at that bit of moisture that somehow always appeared on my cheek when I had these little chats with Cassie. She always got to the heart of me.

"Aggie looks a little odd, don't you think? What *is* it about her that's different?"

"Er…I don't know, sweetie."

"I think it's time we started using the vet in Lanierville—just until Doc White comes back from his vacation. I swear her tail looks four inches shorter. Wonder what they did to her when you weren't looking?"

"I guess we'll never know." I sighed dramatically.

CHAPTER FOURTEEN

"So why do you think Haverstock took off like a scared rabbit? If he's not guilty of something—if that really is cow's shi…er, dung in those little brown bags—then why pull a disappearing act and leave a roomful of pissed off patients just because I arrived on the scene?"

Horatio smiled—although for the merest fraction of a second it seemed like a well-mannered smirk.

"Do you honestly not know how intimidating you can be, my dear? As an outraged mother—on a scale from one to ten, you are way off the chart."

"A virago?"

"Roget couldn't have said it better."

"Thanks. I just used the word in Leonard's latest."

"Umm, somehow that doesn't seem like the language our Leonard is wont to use."

"He has a new sidekick."

"A librarian or a school teacher?"

"Nope. Guess again."

"A writer."

"Yeah," I grinned. "How you'd guess?"

"He did appear to bemoan his solitary state more than usual in your latest tome. I assume this person is of the feminine gender?" he added. "And redheaded?"

We both enjoyed a companionable chuckle. Horatio was well aware that for years I had complained of not being able to take credit for my own blood, sweat and tears. Leonard Paisley was my creation, but it was he who took all the credit for my books. Horatio knew as well as I did that my new literary lady friend would be my way of "if you can't beat 'em, join 'em."

"So, you think Haverstock is nothing more than a chicken-hearted little turd who thinks he's God's gift to women?"

Horatio took a long puff on his pipe and carefully exhaled a perfect circle of wobbly white smoke the size of a cantaloupe. "Hummm."

I could get nothing more out of him, but I did notice that he was biting down on the pipe stem hard enough to bare his right incisor.

We both sat there ruminating until I fell asleep. When I woke up about an hour later his chair was empty.

After a satisfying stretch or two, I wandered around the house looking for somebody to bug. For some reason I was inexplicable lonely and when I saw Cassie and her dog on the back porch I made a beeline straight for her.

"How long did you think you could get away with it, Mom?"

My smile drooped and my stomach knotted up in a sudden cramp. My dirty secret was out. Cassie loved that wicked little pooch, and I felt lower than the lying worm I was and hated myself for not fessin' up when I had the chance to convince her that pulling all the long hair out of the dog's tail was just an accident. Now, no matter what I said, it would just look like a stupid excuse.

"Cassie…"

"Did you think I wouldn't find out?"

"I…no. I guess not, honey, but…"

"And what really hurts is that you of all people—my own mother—thinks I'm really such loser that I can't get a date on my own?"

"Wha…what are you talking about?"

"You know very well what I'm talking about!"

"No, I don't. I thought you were mad about Aggie. You've got me confused."

"What about Aggie?" demanded my tall avenging daughter as she swirled around to confront me face to face.

"Her tail…"

"I know all about her tail. That stupid vet pulled out her beautiful tail just to get back at me for showing him the door. And don't think I'm not going to make a complaint to the State Veterinary Association! I'm going to demand they yank his temporary license to practice in this country. But that's not the point! I'm mad because you and Gran are trying to fix me up with one of her old crony's grandsons. As if you didn't know," she added with a distinctly unlady-like snort." She plopped dramatically down on the chaise. I closed my eyes for a moment when I heard the ominous creak, but when I opened them again she and the chaise were none the worse for wear.

"In the first place…"

"You're just as meddling and nosey as Gran and that silly old Mavis Madden. Imagine! How in the world could she even begin to think I would go out on a blind date with that insane woman's progeny. There's got to be a piece missing off every one of that queer woman's chromosomes. Does Gran believe that her spawn could escape those demented genes?"

"Step-grandson."

"And have you forgotten the day Mavis smacked poor little Aggie?"

"*Step*-grandson, Cassie."

"Step…you mean he's not a blood relative?"

"No, he's not. He grew up in Atlanta and graduated from Emory three years before you did."

"Well, maybe…no! I still don't like being tricked. And I hate blind dates. No, no, no," she wailed. "The answer is no!"

And I was left alone and abandoned once again.

CHAPTER FIFTEEN

The next morning dawned bright and windy. Cassie had left before I got up and Mother and Horatio announced at breakfast they intended a trip to Wieuca City to investigate new light fixtures for the porch and patio. Alone again.

Rather than hang around the house and feel guilty about not working on Leonard's latest, I decided to drive down to the lakes and hang out there for the day—under the guise of research for "local color." The wind picked up as I got closer to the dam and when I crossed over the road on top of the spillways I could see the waves splashing against the shore.

With red warning flags flapping wildly overhead and spray sparkling in the sunshine, I could see why only a very few of the bigger boats dared venture onto the water. No fish, I decided, would be worth going out in that, and I changed my plans to go have "fresh catch" lunch at Catfish Pond. No sense in asking for trouble for anyone, fishermen included.

I drove in and out of the narrow roads leading to rough pebble strewn beaches for a couple of hours looking for a sheltered place to park and ruminate, but everywhere I turned the wind blustered and blew—making my plans to sit on a picnic table and watch the world go by impossibly uncomfortable.

I finally gave up on my fruitless quest and decided maybe the glassed-in dining room at Foxtrot Charlie's might afford a respite from the weather and still allow a view of the lake.

From a lovely corner table in front of a big glass window I ordered another grilled chicken salad, and just to keep my hand in—added steak fries. Grinning broadly at nothing at all but my audacity in combining what was good for me and what was not, I sipped on a truly delicious mint iced tea and watched foolhardy yachtsmen hurriedly load their boats back up on trailers and head for home.

Somehow during my sipping and grinning, the picture of Andy's face suddenly came to mind. "Leave this case alone," he had said. And then he had ominously added something about "more than meets the eye" and "it's dangerous."

Goosebumps suddenly appeared on my forearms, and I shook them off with an effort. "Nonsense," I muttered under my breath. Bags of cow poo and a little faux Englishman who thought he was God's gift to women weren't in the least bit frightening. Stupid and silly, maybe, but scary?

But there was something about the not so good doctor that raised my hackles. There was something about him … something that tickled my memory. But try as I might nothing came to me before my gorgeously overflowing salad was served, and after that I forgot everything but my appetite. I dug in and ate my way happily to the bottom of the bowl, completely forgetting the fries until they were limp and unappealing.

Feeling virtuous and fat-free, I stopped at the wonderful new cupcake bakery on the way home and got a half-dozen of the flavors of the week, devouring one extra—a delicious bananas foster on the way home.

The driveway was empty when I arrived, and Aggie didn't even ask to go out when I entered the house. I figured Cassie must have come and gone again. There was no note on the kitchen table to let me know the whereabouts of my kith and kin, but the answering machine was blinking wildly.

"Paisley. It's Trudy. From the library," she added unnecessarily. "You dropped a couple of microfiche behind the cabinet. I wondered if you had missed seeing them and wanted to come back. Or maybe it's not important. Either way, they'll be on my desk for a day or two. See you soon," she added gaily, and hung up.

The nice little nap my full tummy was yearning for began to disappear into the distance as curiosity loomed large on the horizon. Two more files, two more possibilities. The hope of finding out even the tiniest tidbit that might spread some light on the mysterious marks on Millicent's withered skin made getting back in my car and driving to the library a small price to pay.

"Wow," beamed Trudy, "you didn't waste any time. I'm getting curious, Paisley. Working on a new book?"

"Maybe, just maybe," I told her, adding under my breath, "If I'm lucky, and Billy is luckier."

CHAPTER SIXTEEN

It was obvious that Trudy, or some of her helpers, had been busy down in the basement. The dust of years and years had been impossible to completely remove, but the surfaces were a good deal cleaner and smelled pleasantly of disinfectant and furniture wax.

The microfiche reader even sported a new bulb and started humming immediately when I turned it on. I still didn't know what I was looking for, but I scanned every inch of the ancient newspaper clippings with a fresh eye and was quickly rewarded with a curious story on page three of the March 3, 1954, edition of the *Lakeland County Times*.

SECOND SISTER SUCCUMBS
TO UNKNOWN CAUSES

Abigail Poole succumbed earlier this week at Lanierville General Hospital, apparently to the same unknown disease process that killed her younger sister last month. Eliza Poole died February 13th of this year.

The doctors who attended both young girls admit they are somewhat mystified as to the cause of death but wish to assure the public that there does not seem to be any contagion in the offing. Both of the sisters were good students, and while somewhat reticent and shy, were well liked by their peers at Saint Anthony's Academy. They lived with their father, James Arthur Poole, at 312 Market Street in Rowan Springs, their mother, the former Hannah Haygood of Wieuca City, having died in childbirth several years previously."

As I read the article I realized that my initial excitement was ill placed. The date was right, but no "m's," or "n's," or even "w's." I imagined lots of people died of unknown causes back in the fifties, especially in a little town where autopsies would be considered a rarity and not the norm.

Since no one was there to see or hear, I didn't even bother to suppress a huge yawn and issued an indelicate and slightly banana flavored burp before I scrolled to the next page. Fifteen minutes later I came across a follow up to the story I had just dismissed.

MYSTERY DEEPENS IN
SISTERS' DEATHS

Authorities are looking into the strange deaths of two young girls in our community. Sisters Abigail and Eliza Poole, daughters of Mr. James Arthur Poole of Rowan Springs, died early this year of mysterious causes. Medical doctors working on the cases professed puzzlement over the strange symptoms present in both young girls before they weakened and succumbed to illness.

Teachers at Saint Anthony's Academy reported Eliza Poole left school several times during the month previous to her death complaining of strange pains in the abdomen. She was reported as "pale and shaking" on more than one occasion and while neither her father, nor the live-in housekeeper took the girl to the doctor, she appeared to have overcome her symptoms for a period of time. On the day of her death, she attended school as always, but that same afternoon the housekeeper could not rouse her after a nap.

The doctor on call at the local clinic pronounced her at home. She was thought to have died of natural causes. A congenital heart defect was suggested.

Miss Abigail Poole's illness took a quicker course. She was rushed to Lanierville General Hospital after suffering much the same symptoms, albeit much more severe, and was pronounced dead on arrival on at that hospital.

Because of the mysterious nature of the deaths, laboratory studies are being performed on samples taken from both young women. Results are pending.

"Well," I whispered. "The game seems to be afoot!"

Barely suppressing my excitement, I hurriedly changed the microfiche and quickly scanned the second one. Immediately, the much larger headlines jumped out at me:

MURDER IN ROWAN SPRINGS?

Outside Investigators have been called in to view the evidence in the recent deaths of two young women who resided with their father at 312 Market Street. The father, James Arthur Poole, had been invited to answer questions on several occasions, but so far has not been able to shed any light on the case. He denied the allegations of some of his neighbors who stated that he had been having inappropriate relations with his live-in housekeeper, Mrs. Margaret Nance Whitelaw, a widow, who had moved in when his wife passed away. The two girls had, on occasion, confided to school mates that Mrs. Whitelaw was trying to "take their mother's place" in the home."

Mrs. Whitelaw, so far, has refused to talk to the authorities.

Laboratory studies performed during the last month have reportedly raised some disturbing questions but police have not divulged any further information. Anyone having knowledge of these mysterious incidents is asked to come forward. Please contact the Rowan Springs Police Department from 8-5pm on week days at telephone number 2224.

"Wow!" I whispered, and "wow!" again. I had found the initials I was looking for, and I had not one, but two mysterious deaths, and two new leads. One, the police chief in 1954—if he was still alive—and if not, the police archives; and two, the name of the housekeeper—and maybe mistress of Mr. James Arthur Poole. It wasn't until that afternoon when I was crowing to Horatio about my endeavors that he informed me I had more than that: the address of the deceased girls, and therefore the neighbors, and the school where they were students.

CHAPTER SEVENTEEN

"Torn down?"

"'Fraid so, my dear. About ten years ago according to the city records. Something about a Quickie Mart."

"Stupid Quickie Mart!"

I thought for a moment. "The neighbors?" I ventured hopefully.

"Parking lot."

"The school?"

"Mini-mall."

"Rats!"

"Indeed," added Horatio somewhat absently.

We were alone in the library waiting for Mother to finished getting dressed for their "date night." Horatio had already confided to me the nature of the "something special" he had planned for his beloved Anna, and I could hardly wait until the next morning to learn what her take on his surprise might be.

But I was itchy with an uneasy feeling that went well beyond my curiosity to see how Mother liked her fancy dinner on the casino riverboat. Not to mention the fact that Horatio had been less than enthusiastic about my hastily made conclusions concerning the Poole sisters. I was sure they had been murdered and he was not.

"Lead poisoning, most likely," he surmised. "The case was dismissed for lack of evidence, after all. Too bad the house was torn down. But it's a given those old walls were thick with layers of lead based paint. Built in the early part of the century, the clerk said. Lead paint for certain. Waste your time elsewhere, my dear."

Of course, that last statement made me more determined than ever to "waste as much time" as I wanted to in order to prove my case. I made a mental note to look up the symptoms of lead poisoning when they had left, and added as an afterthought, the arsenic which he had so readily dismissed.

"If the shoe fits…," I murmured as I read the information on arsenic. I was certain it was murder and that I had found the murder weapon, the murderess, *and* the scene of the crime. What I didn't know was how Millicent figured into the puzzle. But I truly believed that she did somehow and had painfully carved the perpetrator's initials in her own skin for some bizarre reason that made perfect sense to her alone.

I printed out the most pertinent information on arsenic—meaning that which made my hypothesis more believable, and fell asleep on the sofa in the library with the papers sliding off my chest onto the floor.

It was late and very dark when Horatio and mother returned, but the happy lady was so full of joy and enthusiasm from her "surprise" that I couldn't help but rouse and smile as she related their evening.

"…and the food, Paisley dear, simply divine. And beautifully served, I might add, which is so rare these days, as you know. Do you even remember all the delicacies, Horatio darling? I can't," she continued. "There were simply too many…oh, that succulent shrimp dish, and something with *crème fraiche*. You simply have to make reservations and take Cassie, my dear. Oh, and I won! Can you imagine?"

"I thought you didn't approve…"

"Oh, don't be so old-fashioned, dear. It's perfectly legitimate these days. Tell her, Horatio. You wouldn't have suggested it otherwise, would you, dear. Paisley, I'm ashamed you would even think such a thing about dear Horatio! It's not a dive, darling, or a speakeasy," she added with a theatrical shudder.

"But I didn't…"

"Not in so many words, but your tone…"

"Nightcap, anyone?" interrupted the ever diplomatic Mr. Horatio Raleigh.

"No thank you, sweetheart," cried mother gaily. "I think I'll divest myself of these raiments and get ready for bed." She gave me a quick peek on the cheek and patted Horatio's softly. "You'll be there shortly, won't you, darling," she added meaningfully and floated out of the room.

"Looks like you got lucky," I noted slyly.

"Paisley!" admonished the dear man, blushing profusely. "Here, take your sherry. And what are all these papers on the floor?"

"Oh, right!" I sputtered over a mouthful. "Information on arsenic poisoning. Fits all the symptoms of the Poole children's illnesses."

"You mean you made them fit to suit your sketchy facts. I thought you had learned over the span of your brief lifetime as a pseudo-detective to be more clinical in your approach. I'm surprised that you are so determined to make a silk purse out of a sow's ear, so to speak."

"Wow! Talking about mixed metaphors."

"Well, it's late, and I'm somewhat tired."

"Not too tired, I hope. After all, your lady awaits."

"Hmmpf!" he muttered as he downed the last of a very good sherry. "See you tomorrow, missy," and left the room, trying without much success to hide a very satisfied smile.

For a very brief minute I allowed myself to ruminate on the sad state of my love life, meaning none at all. But that meant not celebrating the fact that Mother and Horatio had finally managed to share their love, and I was not going to allow myself that selfishness.

"Hooray for them!" I whispered softly.

CHAPTER EIGHTEEN

Billy Arlequin had been in the Lakeland County jail for almost a month now, and he seemed quiet and very resigned to his fate—almost pathologically so. I asked him why after I seated myself on the folding chair the assistant jailor had grudgingly brought out of musty old closet.

"What's up with that?" I asked, trying to jar him out of his state of ennui.

"Go away, Mrs. DeLeon," he sighed. "It's hopeless, my case, I mean, come on…my styling scissors poking out of her neck? And all that blood!" He shuddered violently and tears filled his eyes.

I got up and looked underneath the flimsy metal chair to give him a moment to compose himself. Using the tips of my fingers, I carefully brushed away several spider webs and egg sacs trying not to show my own feelings of disgust. I hated spiders.

"Look, Billy, I know it's awful being in jail. I was here once, and I'll never forget."

He looked up sharply. His face now a stoic mask. "You were?"

"Yup! Trespassing. And I scared an old lady half outta her wits. And I believe I tried to resist arrest."

"Goodness," he laughed. It sounded good. "You—a hardened criminal? I would never have guessed it. You seem all meek like and quiet."

I sat still for a moment while his description of me sank in.

"That's not exactly what I'm aiming for, but never mind."

"Well, no offense and all, but I sure can't picture a lady like you sitting on this side of the bars."

"Well, thank you, I guess. But let me ask a few questions before they kick me out of here. We only have twenty minutes."

Perking up somewhat, he turned around on the cot and faced me squarely. He was a small man, probably not much taller then I was. A month in jail had increased what I imagined was a natural pallor, and his stringy black hair belied his trade. The orange over-alls they had given him to wear hung loosely on his wiry frame and increased the unhealthy aspect of his pale complexion. Billy Arle-quin looked almost as frail as the lady he was accused of killing.

"Did you ever notice anything unusual about Millicent?"

"Ha! You'd need all day for the answer to that question, forget twenty minutes!"

"I mean her person, her body…specifically her skin?"

"You mean all dried up and wrinkly? Yeah, well, I rubbed her down with some very expensive creams at least once a week and more often in cold weather. She claimed it hurt sometimes she was so dry. I always tried to make her as comfortable as I could." He thought for a minute and added hastily, "But never in her private parts, if you know what I mean."

"Nobody has accused you of being inappropriate, Billy."

"No," he scoffed, "just murder."

I spent almost a half hour with the prisoner, but got no more information out of him. It was as if he were so afraid of saying something that might sound incriminating that he wouldn't say anything at all—even to save his hide. He must have realized from the get go that his entire relationship with the Millicent Grazian-ni—a practically penniless younger man caretaking a wealthy and much older woman—would be deemed by most folks in our fair town as "inappropriate."

My visit did seem to have done him some good, though, and I was happy for that. And I took heart in the fact that he did promise to think about "things" that might help his case and let me know if he came up with something. I was even more convinced that whatever happened to Millicent, bizarre accident or premeditated murder—Billy was innocent.

I had invited Cassie to meet me at the Dairy Queen for lunch, but she declined at the last minute, sending me a text with the bad news.

"Damn technology," I muttered over the large salad I had or-dered in anticipation of her approval of my healthy choice off a menu loaded with things I would much rather eat. Phone texts were all fine and good if one were too busy to call, but a daughter de-clining a mother's invitation seemed to warrant a short voicemail message at the very least. I was sure it was because she didn't want to speak to me.

She was hiding something. And I knew it!

It didn't take long to glean the information out of Mother. She was so proud of herself for coming up with the idea in the first place, she was positively beaming when she confided in me the secret that I was certain Cassie had made her swear to keep to herself.

"He's adorable, Paisley," she enthused. "Good looking does not half do him credit, and we know he's smart to have graduated *cum laude* from Emory. Owns his own company and he's only three years older than our precious Cassie. He's perfect, simply perfect!"

"Well, there is the Madden factor…"

"Pish and tush!" she remarked dismissively. I smiled, noticing that she had picked up Horatio's speech mannerisms.

"So her first husband's ex-wife's step-daughter is his mother, so what! I'm sure we would never have even known about him if he hadn't moved back in the vicinity and been such a hottie."

I laughed at her new word and she had the decency to blush "Why, Mother, you're positively waxing poetic about the young man," I teased.

"Well, it's high time our sweet baby found someone who deserved to be graced with her company. She's been practically slumming for the last few years."

Mother was so obviously pleased with this new turn of events that I decided not to remind her that Mavis Madden was famous for grabbing any and all opportunities to shine—something she had few chances to do of late. I could see her now inserting herself and her hare-brained husband at our Thanksgiving dinner table as representatives of Cassie's new family. I shuddered not once but twice, and then a third time at the thought of listening to her shrill voice over my plate of mashed potatoes, peas and turkey. I could only hope that this latest addition to the "adorable" file would be shot down like all the rest. Cassie had very discerning taste. I felt certain I could count on her.

CHAPTER NINETEEN

"You're kidding!" I stammered, flabbergasted. "Please say you're kidding," I added, hoping my voice didn't sound as needy and whiny to her as it did to me. "I mean, you can't be serious," I managed in a more brisk and authoritative tone.

My daughter looked down at me from her considerable height in the four-inch stiletto's she had recently purchased. "He's tall, Mom! Do you know what that means for an Amazon like me?"

"Ha, you're no …."

"You have no idea how it feels to date shorter guys all the time. Munchkins, practically!"

"Well, lately you did …"

"I know, I know, but that wasn't a real relationship and you know it. That was purely for the cause. This…this is different."

"How different?" I asked with my heart in my throat.

"Hmmmm, nice different."

"Damn!" I muttered, vowing to talk mother into a bigger dinner table. Or maybe I could revive the kiddy table and sit there by myself.

"What's that?" she asked suspiciously.

"I said I need to get back to the book."

"Well, happy writing. I'm off to lunch with my new man," she cried gaily, and twirled around on the tips of her toes, her skirt swirling around her like flower petals. She did look lovely…too lovely for her own good.

I was afraid, very afraid.

And I couldn't concentrate long enough to write a sentence. Pam hadn't had to reprimand me of late. In spite of all the time I spent on my real life sleuthing, I had managed to meet her expectations of all my deadlines. Leonard with indeed alive and well and bashing heads and catching bad guys at an alarming rate.

"I need to take a page from my own book," I decided. Another trip to the library was on the offing.

Trudy wasn't there again. Another new substitute assistant librarian pointed me to a stack of open shelving.

"I think they're over there, or maybe on the second row, or maybe that's the later ones. I'm not sure...but somewhere in that general..."

I gratefully turned away when the phone rang and went in search of the older city address books on my own. Miraculously, girl had been right the first time. I found the 1950's section right where she had pointed. I grabbed one of the stepping stools and pulled it over to sit down. It took a while but I finally found the Poole's address. They had apparently moved into the house at 312 Market Street sometime in the early part of 1949. And it was a duplex...actually a triplex as three families shared the house. I had found neighbors...neighbors who were quite close. Close enough to tell me more.

"It was a common thing, my dear," shared Horatio. "During the war older homes were sectioned off and either used as boarding houses or shared rentals—the owners usually relegated to the basement or the attic. Sad, really, when you think about it. What once had been a large and lively family reduced to a single older woman or man who couldn't keep up the cost of owning such a large home on their own and forced to share it—and very often—the single bath, with two, three, or even four other families because of the housing shortage."

"Then they must have been very familiar with one another! Don't you see? If I can contact any one of these people they could possibly, no probably, tell me a lot!"

Horatio sat back in what had now become his chair instead of my father's—not that I minded one bit—and looked over the steeple his long fingers made. "That was very long ago, Paisley. You have to take in account that most of those people have gone to their Maker."

"But they might have had children..."

"Very true," he mused. Do you know the names of the people who lived there? Perhaps I could help you. I buried a considerable number of people in town and my father's records are very detailed. Who do you have on your list, my dear?"

I read off the names of the five different families who had inhabited the big old house on Market Street over the decade or so around the time the Poole children died. Horatio or his father had buried the last of three of them, but he thought the others still had remaining members.

"Of course they could have moved away or sought the services of a funeral home in one of the surrounding counties. A lot of old people have roots out in the country and like to be buried in older churchyards or even family plots.

"I thought you had to be buried in the local cemetery?"

"Not here, my dear. No, it's not against the law to bury a loved one in your backyard, even. All you need is a license from the courthouse."

'You're kidding? You mean that strange bone Aggie found in the backyard last week really could be somebody's great, great uncle?"

"Absolutely. Although in that particular case, I doubt it."

"Why?"

"Too small."

"A child, maybe?"

"Paisley, my dear," he admonished. "You simply have to stop seeing a murder under every bush, so to speak. Believe it or not, most people die in their sleep—or at least of natural causes. People around Rowan Springs are inordinately healthy—some living to a very ripe old age. I suppose the scientific fellows would say it's because of the healthy lifestyle—fresh, homegrown vegetables and fruit, and meat unadulterated with hormones and preservatives. Plenty of exercise and sunshine is the rule for most, and less of the stress and strain that living in a big city engenders. We're a healthy lot."

Fortunately for my purposes, he was right. Three of the children who had spent at least some of their growing up years on Market Street were still around.

CHAPTER TWENTY

"Wild as a March hare!" I mumbled, deep in thought.

"Who's that, dear?"

My mother looked lovely in her tea length rose silk gown.

"Can I help you with those earrings?"

"May, sweetheart. *May* I help you with those earrings. Although I suppose that rough-necked man you spend so much time with doesn't even acknowledge the difference."

My fingernails made little half-moons in the palms of my hand, but I managed to keep a smile on my face. After all, it would do no good to start another fight about Leonard—one I would never win. Especially since she was on her way out, yet again to be wined and dined in grand old Horatio style.

I decided to be snarky instead. "I think Horatio is spoiling you. And remember, *crème fraiche* has bumpdelieshish calories."

"Come now" she smiled gracefully in the mirror. "There is no such word, even for Leonard. And remember, you didn't inherit you tendency to widen through the hips from me. No. It was your dear sweet grandmother Sterling who had to give up her darling little rocker after your father was born for fear of splitting the staves."

"Ehhhh!"

"What's that, dear?"

"Have a good time, Mother."

I trudged back to the library, consoling myself with an extra helping of the wonderful caramel apple cake and a cup of hot cider she had made the night before. Baking was another one of those things she would always do better than anyone, most especially me.

With Mother and Horatio gone, and Cassie out again with the Madden spawn, I was at home alone with the despondent little pup who stayed on my heels until I sat in front of the fire to eat my bounty. She waited for a moment to see if I wanted to share and then hopped up in her favorite spot on the sofa to doze.

I watched the flames from the very realistic gas logs climb up and over the ceramic trunks in never ending new patterns—never once seeing the same flame twice. It was mesmerizing, and I almost dozed off myself.

I'd had a miserable day. It had rained—with a cold wind signaling the coming of winter in a few weeks time. It was still blowing and howling around the corners of the big old house but the library was cozy and warm. I curled up in Horatio's chair with my pad and pencil and set about recording the events of the morning,

An orderly at the State Mental Hospital had immediately directed me to the Administrator's office when I came in—dragging my wet feet and sodden umbrella behind me.

"Right down that hall," he pointed to an open door at the end. "And, hey you!" He added menacingly when I was on my way. "Walk over on the side, if you please. Housekeeping has already been over that floor twice today, and I don't want it all slick and wet again. Some of these patients are a mite unsteady on the feet. Don't want to be responsible for any broken hips, do we! Be more careful in the future."

"Why, of course," I stammered, as he glared down at me. I felt thoroughly chastened and more than a little embarrassed in front of the starchly dressed nurses and aides scurrying about, and I fervently vowed there would be no future visits for me to the State Mental Hospital if I could possibly help it."

My discomfiture increased as I walked into the office at the end of the hall.

"Do you have an appointment?" asked the secretary officiously.

"Why...."

"We must have an appointment, mustn't we? We wouldn't walk into the office of any other busy, busy, busy man without an appointment, would we?"

"I just wanted..."

"We all want things we can't have."

"Look," I raised my voice an octave, "I'm Paisley Sterling, and I want..."

"What you can't have, I know. Like every other selfish, selfish person."

I was getting mad, but I came to the swift realization that the little woman sitting at the desk in front of me was madder still. Her hair was tightly squeezed back in a bun, and her cheeks flamed with artificial color in a wrinkled face powdered as white as snow. Pursed and disapproving lips were painted a brilliant red and her faded blue eyes were rimmed with purple shadow. She looked like a withered and ancient doll sitting ramrod straight in the modern office chair.

"Mrs. Ash," said someone behind me.

I turned and breathed a sigh of relief as a good-looking young man sporting crisply ironed jeans and a smart looking green plaid shirt with a handsome blue tie made his way over to the desk.

Mrs. Ash," he continued. "We've been looking everywhere for you. It's time for morning coffee. You don't want to miss your morning coffee, do you? The kitchen has made those wonderful little buns again. You do love those sugared buns, don't you."

"Why, William," she looked up slightly confused—dazed certainly, and suddenly she lost her belligerence and smiled sweetly. "I think this young lady is here to see you." Her voice regained a little censure as she added, "She doesn't have an appointment."

"That's all right, Mrs. Ash. Don't you worry. I'll make sure she knows all the rules next time."

He turned to the nurse who had followed him. "Jennifer will take you down to the dining room. All the other ladies are waiting for you there."

A smiling Jennifer took the old lady's hand and led her out of sight. "William" sank tiredly down in the chair she had recently vacated and managed a smile for me.

"Sorry about that," he offered. "It's hard to keep up with the ones who are not confined to their rooms or bedridden."

"Seems a great responsibility."

"Well, yeah," he laughed. "It can be trying at times. Sandy's always after me to quit and find something not as, well, *hands on* so to speak. But quite frankly, that's what makes it all worthwhile."

"You enjoy dealing with the half-here and hare-brained?" I asked incredulously.

His fresh and ruddy complexion turned even brighter, standing out in stark contrast to the dark hair combed so neatly off his forehead. "We don't ever…" he stammered.

"I'm sorry!" I interrupted, leaning forward on my hard wooden chair. "I'm a writer. I should know better than to use such offensive language! Please forgive me?"

He looked somewhat mollified. "Well, you …"

"You see I write about this detective who is very rough," I dug deep and tried to remember some of Mother's complaints. "He talks like that, not me."

"I don't understand."

"Leonard Paisley, I write …"

"That's you! Sandy will be over the moon. She loves your books. I'll have to tell her. Would you come to dinner some night? She'll want to brag about it to all her friends."

"Well, I don't usually…"

His complexion returned to the beet red of my previous gaffe. "Of course you don't! Please forgive me for being so forward and naive. Afraid it comes with the territory. I'm so used to being…"

I liked him. I liked him a lot, and I knew my mother, and maybe even Cassie, would adore him. Too bad he was married. This was just the sort of young man who…

It popped out before I had even had time to think it through. "Would you and Sandy like to come to dinner with *us*? At the farm, I mean. Maybe some night next week?"

CHAPTER TWENTY-ONE

"I'm Dr. William Simmons, by the by. Forgive me for not introducing myself right away."

I waved my hand back and forth in a dismissive gesture. "Not a problem. And I do hope you'll come to dinner, but I'm really here to see one of your patients, if that's possible."

"Of course, if they are not indisposed, so to speak. I'm sure they would be glad of the company…especially your company. It's not often we have visitors of any note."

I blushed right on cue and smiled. I liked William more and more each minute.

"Who is it you wish to visit?"

"Mary Alesworthy."

For a second, just a mere second, I saw something furtive behind his eyes, but I blinked and there he was again—all smiles and dimples.

"Hmmm, I don't think we have…," he paused as if ruminating a minute—tapping his cheek with a pencil. "Wait a minute, you mean Jane Alesworthy?"

"I guess so. I don't know her full name."

"Why, we do have Mrs. Jane Alesworthy—have had for quite some time, I'm afraid." He opened a file on his computer and studied it for a moment. "Why, yes indeed. Mary Jane Alesworthy was committed years ago. These old ones who have been here for a so long—I'm afraid we get use to calling them by their given names."

He peered up at me over the computer monitor. "You might not be able to make much sense from any conversation with her, but you're more than welcome to try. She has no next of kin, so I'll have to go through the formalities and ask her permission, but I'm sure she will be delighted to have company."

He pushed back his chair and stood. "Allow me a moment to make sure she's awake and available." He winked. "Won't take a minute. I'll get my real secretary to bring you some tea, if you like?"

I liked, and I liked the tea a lot. Especially since it came with some really good homemade cookies. William was gone more than a minute, and by the time he returned, more than half the plate was empty. I started to apologize for my hearty appetite, but he seemed eager for me to follow him down the hall to the lounge where Jane was waiting so I sneaked another cookie for my pocket and hurried along behind him.

I don't know what I expected, but Mary Jane Alesworthy was more than I could have imagined any little old crazy lady could be. Wrapped from head to foot in three or four long feather boas of green, red, blue and yellow, she sat regally in an armchair with head held high and crowned with a rhinestone tiara.

William stepped back behind me and motioned me forward. He made a slight suggestive bow and, feeling like a complete fool, I followed with a deep curtsey.

"Your Highness," he stated. "This is Paisley of the Rowan Springs Sterlings I spoke to you about. She has come here to pay homage to you."

I turned around to get more clues from him, but he simply gave me a cheeky wink and left me facing the mad queen.

"Please be seated," she said in a quietly regal voice. "You look tired, my dear. Take a load off."

I couldn't help it. I sank down in the overstuffed chair in front of her and laughed. It was a good deep belly laugh, and soon she joined me.

"You must have them really fooled!"

"Have had for years," she giggled. "It's great fun and it passes the time." She leaned closer to me and whispered, "And I do love the costumes, don't you?"

"Absolutely!"

"I don't suppose you have a cigarette? Or a flask on you?"

"Sorry, but I can send something to you when I leave. A care package."

She sighed deeply and looked slightly confused. "Mail? I used to get letters sometimes. And checks! Lots of money—lovely money. But they stopped coming. I don't know why." She suddenly looked sad and forlorn in her feathered finery, and I began to see that she really might not have them fooled all of the time, after all.

"Well, I'll send you a package and call to see if you get it. How about that?"

Something was happening to her. She seemed less and less interested in our conversation and her wrinkled old eyelids began to droop. The dear old thing was falling asleep on me. I had to hurry if I wanted to get anything out of her.

"Jane!"

She looked up, and I could practically see the veil coming down over the faded old eyes. Do you remember living on Market Street? Remember, the big old house with Eliza and Abigail?"

"Oh!" she cried piteously, "The poor mites! How they suffered! And she knew and did nothing about it! Meg knew all about it… she told me. And then there was all that lovely money…" Her words were mumbled, and I leaned forward trying to understand.

I jumped about a foot straight up in the air when Jennifer suddenly appeared at my elbow.

"She's getting tired," she whispered in my ear. "You won't get anything more out of her. She needs to go to her room for a nap. Sorry."

Queen Jane had indeed fallen asleep on her throne. Two orderlies lifted her frail old body into a wheelchair and pushed her away, leaving a few tattered feathers floating in the air in her wake. The interview was obviously at an end.

"Come," ordered Jennifer. "I'll see you out. Dr. Simmons is with an incoming patient. He said to expect a call soon from Sandy. Something about dinner?" She looked hopeful for a moment, like she was expecting me to invite her, but I was too disappointed to feel hospitable so I just followed her to the door and nodded absently when she said goodbye.

CHAPTER TWENTY-TWO

I woke up two hours later, my pad and pencil in heap on the floor in front of me. I unhooked my knees from beneath me and tried to stand up. My legs were all pins and needles and my joints creaked louder than a Chinese emperor's nightingale floor.

I knew it was useless to promise myself a trip to the gym, so I didn't even make the effort. Instead I bent from what seemed a great height and grabbed the pad and pencil from the rug. My pre-nap ramblings were scribbled in the usual hieroglyphics—legible only to me and Leonard. But upon review, I realized my trip to the funny farm might not have been in vain. Maybe Jane did know something about the murders on Market Street so long ago.

"But Horatio!" I wheedled.

"'But' nothing, my dear. She's a dear old lady who has lost her wits and doesn't know where to find them." He chuckled for a moment at his own joke while he filled his pipe.

"You were much more serious about stuff before you married Mother," I grumbled.

"Stuff? What 'stuff' would that be, my dear sweet Paisley."

"The murder stuff. And don't you start with that 'dear sweet Paisley.' You're beginning to sound like Mother when she's trying to change the subject." I stopped and turned around to face him. "Hey! That's exactly what you're doing, right? You've lost interest in this *stuff*, and you don't care anymore about finding out the truth. Mother's got you hogtied and pigtailed and you're happy as clam. And *way* too content to care anymore about poor Billy sitting in jail for something he didn't do."

"Goodness me! Hogs, pigs and clams? All in one sentence. Even the redoubtable Leonard wouldn't indulge in that many creatures in one sentence. And I do take umbrage with your accusations, my dear sweet…um, my sweet."

"Well, it's true!"

I dumped myself down on the sofa in front of the fire and stared glumly into the flames. I'd been doing a lot of that lately and wondered vaguely if I might enjoy the life of a firebug. But that was just plain crazy, and crazy was definitely something I wanted to avoid at all costs.

"I invited him to dinner, you know."

"Who, dear?" asked Mother as she entered the library with a tray of coffee and liquors. "Chartreuse, darling Horatio?" she offered. I noticed there were only two little glasses, and that put me in a worse mood.

"I don't get any?" I groused.

"I didn't think you would want the extra calories, dear," she responded, making my mood even more foul.

"So now all of a sudden I'm on a diet because you and your new husband are at the trough of every calorie-laden restaurant within 50 miles!"

"Why, Paisley! Apologize to Horatio this minute!" She admonished, her face turning a delicate rosy hue. "Horatio simply wants to treat me to some of the finer things in life."

"Like you haven't been enjoying those since the day you were born!"

I flounced out of the library like a spoiled rotten teenager instead of the "mature" woman I was supposed to be. No more naps for me, I decided. I got too grumpy. And I definitely had to apologize to Horatio and Mother for my stupid behavior. But in some ways, I was right. Horatio did appear to have lost a certain amount of interest in Billy's plight—while I had become more and more positive that he was innocent.

CHAPTER TWENTY-THREE

Mother readily, if somewhat absently mindedly, accepted my sincere apology the next morning at breakfast.

"You don't seem to mind very much that I acted like a complete brat," I ventured.

"Oh, that," offered Mother, tearing herself away from a brightly colored travel brochure. "Don't be silly, Paisley, dear. You have those little fits from time to time. I've quite learned to forgive and forget."

I stood there with my mouth open while the steam built up behind my eyes. I was about to blow when Horatio sauntered in the kitchen resplendent in burgundy satin smoking jacket over his pristine white dress shirt and silk tie.

"Morning, my…Paisley. Has Anna told you the delightful news?"

I tamped down the rising anger as curiosity got the better of me.

"No. What? Do tell, Mother." The sarcasm in my voice weighed at least ten pounds.

"We're going on a cruise, dear. To the Bahamas. Isn't that lovely?"

"Bahamas," I croaked. "But what about our mystery, Horatio? Are you just…"

"Forgetting about young Arlequin? No, my child, but until his case comes to court, there's really nothing more I can do."

"The hell you can't!" I burst out. "What about Jane and the other people who lived at the house on Market Street? What about those interviews and…"

"I'm quite certain you can handle all of that admirably without me, my swee…um, Paisley. And I'll—we'll—be back in no time at all. Won't we, Anna, my pet?"

"Well, dear, there is that little side trip we might want to take…"

"No time at all," he repeated, winking at his lady. "No time at all."

And they were off in a cloud of dust before noon, leaving me fuming in the driveway as I waved a reluctant goodbye to the elegant backside of Horatio's Bentley.

"Damn!" I swore loudly and kicked up a pile of gravel with the toe of my already scuffed and dusty loafer. "Damn, and damn again!"

To make matters worse, Sandy Simmons called that afternoon to confirm a date for dinner the next evening.

"I'm so thrilled! Just thrilled to pieces!"

"Yeah, me too."

"So, seven-thirty tomorrow evening, then"

"Yeah."

"Okay, Paisley, bye for now. See you later. Oh! I simply don't know how I'm going to contain myself until then! I'm so excited!"

Cassie was a different story.

"But, Mom! I don't know how to cook!"

"Well, at least you know how to put things together and make them look pretty."

"Like, what things?" she asked suspiciously.

"Fried chicken, and mashed potatoes and things."

"Do not tell me you invited these people to dinner and you're planning to get the food at KFC?"

"Well, if neither of us can cook, what else can we do?"

"Don't you have *any* pride?" I mean you are Anna Howard Sterling Raleigh's daughter. You cannot serve dinner in her beautiful dining room out of a cardboard bucket with paper napkins and plastic forks!"

"Back porch, maybe?"

"It's too chilly in the evenings now, and besides, it's the principle of the thing."

"Then you'll cook?"

"If you'll do the shopping and clean up," she agreed, reluctantly.

I spent the next morning running around Rowan Springs looking for all the things on Cassie's grocery list. It was no mean feat.

"I had to go to Morgantown for that white Mexican cheese," I complained. "What in the world do you need that for? Mother never uses that in any of her recipes."

"Who says anything about Gran's recipes. I don't know anything about her recipes."

I had a sinking feeling in the middle of my stomach. This could be bad, very bad.

"Then whose recipes are you talking about," I ventured cautiously. "Not any of mine—I know that for sure."

"No, Mother, dear. Not yours," she laughed. "Celedia's."

"Celedia! What the hell?"

Celedia had been the cook in the hacienda where we lived in San Romero with Rafe's mother and father. She had been known for her divine cooking for miles around. The DeLeons were proud to have her and treated her like a queen. Cassie had, indeed, spent a great deal of time with her in the kitchen. As a matter of fact, Cassie was the only one allowed in her kitchen. She had quite a majestic attitude as I recalled.

"You mean that stuck-up old woman…?"

"Mom," she warned, shaking a wooden spoon in my face. "She was a delightful lady, and she taught me a lot, I think," she added, a tiny bit of apprehension in her voice.

"You think?"

"Yes! I think. I mean, it was a long time ago, and I was very little, but I do remember certain…things. Like how to make rice."

"Oh, that's just great. Rice. We're having rice. Then what's all this stuff in aid of?" I asked pointing at the piles of grocery goods on the kitchen table.

"Rice, and *carne mechada,* and black beans. Yes, definitely, black beans. And *tres leches torta* for dessert."

She beamed hopefully at me.

"*Tres leches…?*"

"Yep! Three milk cake—the most decadent dessert on the planet."

I didn't have the heart to burst her bubble. The menu sounded simple but it was one that could take hours of preparation and cooking. We had a big job ahead of us.

"Sounds great, honey," I offered with a hug. "Thanks a bunch for doing this."

I was right. Five hours later, every pot, pan, and dish in the kitchen was dirty. The air was full of the stench of burnt rice, and the meat that had been merrily bubbling away on the stove all afternoon was still tough and sinewy.

"Celedia made it look so easy!" she wailed. "I'm sorry, Mom."

Her eyes were bright with unshed tears, and I aimed to make them stay at bay.

"Never mind, pumpkin. That last batch of rice is perfect, well, almost perfect…"

"Thank, God," she choked. "That was the last of it. And there's no time to go and get more."

"Well, it's certainly passable, and so what if the meat is a little tough. It tastes great. And the beans are spot on."

"That's because they came right out of a can."

"Can, smam. Who cares? It's all okay. And the dining room looks beautiful. That counts for a lot, you know."

"Yes," she brightened up. "And these people are not coming for the food, are they? They are mostly interested in my famous writer mother."

"Yeah, well…"

CHAPTER TWENTY-FOUR

And Cassie was right. Not that the dinner wasn't a culinary success, well, almost—but Sandy Simmons was coo-coo for Leonard Paisley and told me so a million times.

"And *Virtual Violence,* wow! That was the most thrilling book ever! Leonard is so virile, don't you think, William?"

"Huh?"

William was too busy ogling my beautiful daughter to pay attention to anything else. I was about to kick him surreptitiously under the table when Sandy repeated,

"Virile, Leonard Paisley?" She looked vexed. "Brother, mine, are you not listening to a word we've been saying?"

Brother? And that put a whole new light on things.

"Here William," I offered with the brightest smile I could muster, "Have another piece of this delicious cake. Cassie made it with her own two hands."

So he ate two more pieces of cake while making eyes at my baby.

Sandy offered to help me clean up, but I was afraid if she saw the state the kitchen was in, she might want to run to the emergency room of the nearest hospital to have her stomach pumped, so she and I sat in the library while she prattled on about Leonard. She was older than William—maybe four or five years, and not nearly so attractive. They had the same dark hair but hers was turning grey and her once pretty face was pudgy and sagged—like the rest of her. But it wasn't hard to see that as much as she professed to love Leonard Paisley, she really thought the sun came up for her brother.

Cassie and William had disappeared outside, presumably to walk Aggie. But they were gone much longer than it usually took for Aggie's needs to be met and when they returned, the color was high in Cassie's cheeks.

Somehow that didn't sit right with me. Too soon, I thought, for any amorous shenanigans. I yawned hugely, hoping they would take a hint.

"We must be going," said Sandy, immediately. "We taken up too much of your precious time as it is."

"Oh, no," I lied. "We've enjoyed every minute."

"Every minute when you could have been writing!"

"Oh, Mom doesn't write after…"

"We must do this again sometime," I interrupted. "Sometime when Mother and Horatio are home."

"Yes," William responded. "I've heard so much about Mr. Horatio Raleigh. I'm anxious to see if I think some of those stories are true."

Rather odd way of putting it, I thought, but they were both really so pleasant and appreciative, and I was so glad to see the last of them, I let the thought drift away on the bubbles surrounding the dishes in the sink.

"My word! It will take you two hours or more to clean up all this mess," noted Cassie. "Well, goodnight."

CHAPTER TWENTY-FIVE

It did, indeed, take two hours—almost exactly as a matter of fact, to get the kitchen squeaky clean. But it would have taken less time if I hadn't spent most of it picking goat feathers, as my grandmother Howard used to say. I took the extra time to revisit everything I remembered about Millicent's death.

Billy was innocent. I had accepted that as the truth and nothing else I had come up with seemed to sway me from that decision. Of course, his hair styling scissors sticking out of her bloody neck might pose a big problem for a jury; but it was up to me, I now realized, to counter that with something big. Something that would keep him from the courtroom in the first place.

The visit to the State Hospital had been a disappointment: an old lady's demented ramblings down memory lane had taken a detour for sure. And now I didn't know where else to turn.

I laughed at that bit of nonsense and blew some of the bubbles my vigorous efforts had created up into the air above the sink. Washing dishes, I decided, was good for the soul and the brain. I did not, however, want to make a habit of it.

William Simmons posed a problem. Cassie hadn't said a word about the evening, but I was fairly certain she liked him. She didn't go all pink cheeked and girlish giggles over just anyone. And the more I thought about it—she never went all pink cheeked and giggles at all. I definitely had to ask her about that in the morning.

When I finished washing the dishes and mopping greasy spots off the floor, I put away the multitude of cooking utensils we had used and took a cup of tea to the library. To my surprise, Cassie and Aggie were sitting in front of the fire waiting for me.

"You know," I ventured, "two more hands would have made a lighter task."

"I cooked. You cleaned."

I laughed. "We did indeed. And by the way, thanks."

"Welcome."

"I think they actually enjoyed it."

"Maybe"

"Okay, what's up with you? Did William pull some funny stuff while you two were outside?"

Ignoring my question, she turned to face me. "Is there something wrong with me? I mean, do I attract nothing but weirdoes and losers? You always seemed to pull in the nice guys—a bit wild and woolly, risk-takers, spies—that sort of thing—but heroes. Not exactly keepers, but really decent sorts you could be proud of."

She turned to gaze back in the fire and ruffled Aggie's fluffy white hair.

I held my breath. Aggie never really bit her mistress—badly, that is. But there was always a first time.

I didn't answer for a while, thinking about her question. I knew the answer was important to her—not something I could just pull quickly out of the mommy hat. This was a heart to heart question and deserved a good honest answer.

"I don't know, honey."

"That's all you can come up with?"

She turned her startled face to me and bounded up and onto the sofa. Aggie jumped into her lap, and after turning around two times, sank down for another nap.

"I mean, this is serious, Mom." Tears hovered behind luminous dark eyes, and I struggled to come up with a better answer. I couldn't.

"I'm sorry," I began. "I really don't know." She started to get up and Aggie jumped down in alarm—ready to follow her mistress anywhere.

"Now wait!" I called. "I'm not finished. Give me another chance."

"Well, okay," she said, plopping back down with Aggie again.

"It's something I worried about myself, too."

"About me?"

"No. About me. About all those so-called *heroes*. Maybe they weren't so great, after all. Of course, at first your father seemed so nice and safe. I was sure we would have a nice, quiet, comfortable life together. Live in suburbia, get a dog, raise kids—certainly grow old together. I never dreamed on the life we led."

"You didn't know you were going to live in San Romero when you got married?"

She seemed truly surprised. So, I realized, was I.

"No! Not at all. He got a job at the university analyzing core samples in the geology lab, and I played the typical suburban house-wife who cleaned the house, took care of the baby, and had dinner ready when hubby came home. Nice and quiet and placid—and well, dull, if you must know. I have to admit I was excited when he first proposed moving to San Romero and taking up the diplomatic post he had been offered. But it was totally unexpected."

I started dreamily into the fire, remembering those exciting days, when so in love, I never once questioned the wisdom of mov-ing to a foreign country with a small child and forgoing all that I knew and loved.

"How about Gran and Grandaddy? How did they react?"

"They were all for it, as I remember. Of course, I know now that they were brokenhearted when I moved and took you so far away."

"Would you have stayed had you known?"

"I doubt it. Rafe was my world. I would have followed him anywhere."

"Wow."

"Yeah," I responded sourly. "Wow."

I answered the rest of her questions about our early life in San Romero by rote, my mind deep in memories of happy times—the beautiful music of Spanish guitars—me swaying in the arms of my dashing husband as we danced the night away on the large patio of our hacienda home…

"Mom!"

"Uh, yeah?"

"You said the same thing twice in the last two minutes."

"Sorry, honey. What's that?"

"That you loved Daddy."

My heart skipped a beat and quick tears flooded my eyes. I didn't allow myself these thoughts very often. These were memo-ries I had tucked in the deep recesses of my mind—there to stay, jealously guarded—too precious to dwell upon.

My sweet daughter immediately moved from the sofa to sit on the floor beside my chair and hold my hand.

"I'm so sorry, Mommy. I didn't mean to make you cry. It was a terrible, terrible thing that happened to you, and I didn't mean to make you…"

"Remember that your father went missing in the jungle and we had to flee for our lives?"

"Well, yes," she answered, biting on her lower lip. "That."

I wiped the tears from my face and tried to smile.

"It's my fault. You asked a question about you, and I went on prattling about me. I'm a totally self absorbed…"

"Nonsense! And forget I asked the stupid question in the first place. How about another piece of *tres leche?* A midnight snack just for you and me."

I laughed. It felt good. Why couldn't I remember that before I started doing things that were bound to make me sad?

"We can't. William ate it all."

"Stupid William."

"And speaking of Mr. Perfect—what happened with William in the moonlight?"

CHAPTER TWENTY-SIX

"I don't know," she answered.

"There seems to be a lot of that going around." I laughed. "If you don't want…"

"No, no, I don't mind telling you anything—well, almost anything; but we talked, of course. And then he began to come on to me. Flirting outrageously. 'I was so beautiful. I was so smart. I was *such* a good cook.'"

"No wonder you were giggling."

"Now, Mom. I got the job done, didn't I?"

"Well, except for the last one, all the things he said were true and it's not such a rare thing for a potential suitor to tell you so."

"Potential suitor? I think not!"

"But he's so good looking and such a nice dresser. He's got to be smart to hold down the position he does, and most of all—he's not related to Mavis Madden."

"Maybe not, but he's just a little bit too peculiar for me."

"Peculiar?" I asked, instantly seeing some of the things that happened at the hospital in a new light.

"To put it in Leonard's vernacular, 'queer as a two dollar bill.'"

"Queer?"

"Yes. Strange, and just a smidge creepy."

"Creepy?"

"Mom, you're beginning to sound like a parrot."

"How so? And don't say, 'I don't know.'"

She lay down on the floor, deposited Aggie upside-down on her chest and began to rub the dog's little pink tummy.

"Cassie, I wouldn't do that if I were you."

"Well, you're not me—we've established that a long time ago, and beside—she loves it."

The dog, indeed seemed to be in high heaven—her eyes closed and her tail wagging upside down slowly in blissful relaxation. It was a truly frightening sight.

"Oh, well, you know best."

"I do," she stated vehemently. "And I know when a guy is creepy because that seems to be all the ones I attract. Moth to a flame," she observed sadly, looking into the fire.

"That's not true! Look at what's his name—Bert's son…"

"You mean the one who went to Afghanistan on some 'funny business' that had nothing to do with the military, and hasn't been heard of since? How normal is that?'"

"Well, yeah, there is that. But he was very nice when you were dating. And how about that young man from Emory you went to Europe with…"

"David who was arrested in Spain for bringing in pot? Just how normal and grown-up is that? I mean, carrying ten ounces of marijuana on a backpacking trip around the world. My word! How stupid can you get?"

"Have you heard from him lately?" I asked quietly.

"Yeah, we email back and forth all the time. Apparently prison is not so bad. He was a business major, after all, and he has this little scam going. Seems to be doing quite well."

I laughed until she did, and the room seemed suddenly brighter and warmer—old ghosts banished to another place and another time.

"Back to William." I prodded. "Just what was creepy about him?"

"You know when you see a big old spider—how you skin gets all tingly and crawly?"

I did indeed. Just thinking about it made me shudder. Spiders were not my favorite thing.

"Well, that's how I felt when he touched me. It was strange, too, 'cause like you said, he is good looking—and smart. In the grand scheme of things I ought to be overjoyed that he likes me. I mean, what a catch—huh? What's wrong with me, Mom?"

"In the grand scheme of things, absolutely nothing."

"You're my mom, and you have to say that."

"Let me finish. Like I was saying—nothing is wrong, but you are picky…"

"Now, just a darn minute!"

"*Very picky*, as well you should be. There are a lot of crazies out there on the prowl, and you have to be aware and protect yourself. I think because of your background in San Romero and the scary things you went through, you have a very highly developed sense of self-protection that many young women lack. The unprepared become easy prey for the less than decent sorts that seem to abound in our world today. Be careful, Cassie," I warned. "Listen to that little voice who calls out 'creepy' every time you hear it. It will serve you well."

CHAPTER TWENTY-SEVEN

Cassie appeared to heed my advice. She refused to take the calls that William made to the farm all morning long. First I told him she went to town, and then that she was washing her hair, and finally I just quit answering the phone.

But when around two o'clock in the afternoon a florist van pulled up in the driveway and the driver deposited a beautiful vase with two dozen red roses on the back porch, she began to re-think her decision.

"Maybe I was just tired. Maybe he's not so creepy after all. And he is so good looking…"

And before I could say, 'Jack's your uncle,' they had made a date for Saturday night.

"So, where you going?" I asked, a bit miffed that she had been persuaded from her original point of view so easily.

"Ummm, I'm not exactly sure. He said he wanted to get tickets for *Les Miserables,* but it might be too late. And besides he doesn't think so much of small town players. He says the Broadway show would be better for me to see the first time."

"And he, no doubt, wants to take you to New York to see the play there? All that way just to see *Les Miserables*?"

"Well, that and other things," she answered, a dreamy look on her lovely face.

"It's the 'other things' I have a problem with," I mumbled.

We got some postcards from Mother and Horatio in the mail. Scenes of the beautiful sea and lovely sky and perfect white sandy beaches where they had decided to spend a romantic interlude. For a moment that old jealousy sneaked up behind me and whacked me in the heart—yearning searing my lonely soul; but I threw the cards down on the kitchen table for Cassie to see and grabbed my jacket. Time for a drive down to the lake to clear out the cobwebs and cleanse the soul. I had no time for a could-a-been, or what-if.

The wind was high, but not as high, or as dangerous as it had been on my last visit, so I drove down to the waters edge and found a spot overlooking Teddy Creek Bay. The sun was shining brilliantly overhead, causing the white hulls of the little sailboats to gleam brightly against the dark water of the lake. Fishermen trawled around the edges of the bay, stopping at decent intervals to pull up their heavy nets, full of the 'catch of the day.' It was a beautiful sight. Who needed to go to some stupid old beach in the Bahamas, I thought? We have it all right here.

Ruminating on the 'catch of the day' made me realize I had skipped breakfast. I was really hungry now that my little pity party was over, and I needed food fast, but not fast food. I bounced my little car back over the rocks and pebbles on the beach, taking no heed of the advice of the last mechanic who had told me to, "Take it easy. You're not driving a tank, you know!" and headed for the closest place serving fresh fish.

I was seated in a comfortable corner booth, once again over-looking the lake and all its beauty, when I had an unexpected visitor.

"Well, looky here, how lucky can a mate get? Lunch with a good looking sheila like Paisley Sterling. Can't get any better than that—unless it's with her lovely scheming little daughter."

He slid into the bench opposite me, grinning like a shark from the old Merrrie Melody cartoon movies. I was immediately aware of the fact that he was more than a little tipsy. His breath stank of bourbon and he looked like he had slept in his clothes. I was furious.

"I think you'd better leave before I make a scene," I whispered loudly. "The owner's a friend of mine," I lied. "He'll kick you out in a second if I say so."

"I think not, Paisley love. Because Mick is a friend of mine. Just bought the place last month, as a matter of fact. Turning it into a 'shrimp on the Barbie' franchise this summer, he is. With me as one of them fancy financiers."

I must have turned a tad pale because he took great pleasure in continuing, "Didn't expect that, did you, love? Me owning a piece of 'your friend's' restaurant?"

"No," I stammered, "my mistake…"

"You mean *your lie*, don't you, love," he added in a nasty voice.

"Yes, my lie," I admitted. "But your lie is bigger than mine. Veterinarian, my hind foot! That's a much bigger lie any day. It may even be fraud…and practicing medicine without a license is a crime! You are up to no good, admit it!"

My voice had raised an octave, and the few remaining late lunch guests were staring at the corner booth with fascination.

He sat back and grinned—self-satisfaction plumping out the new hollows in his cheeks and making him appear somewhat handsome again. The dark circles beneath his eyes were almost hidden behind the expensive aviator sunglasses, and his sallow skin looked healthier in the late afternoon light. But it was still easy to see that Huntley Haverstock had seen some rough days lately, and I would bet, even rougher nights.

"But I *am* a vet," he said with a Cheshire cat smile. "A real vet with a real license and all the trimmings. You can check, if you like, with Immigration. All the necessary papers signed, sealed and delivered to your government and mine. *Bonafied*, I am," he boasted. "*Bonafied*!"

The declaration seemed to take all the steam out of him. His head began to droop and the fresh and feisty look melted away like wax exposed to a flame. Huntley Haverstock was ill. I told him so.

"Not ill," he differed sadly. "Just sick. Sick and tired of hate and revenge and a life wasted trying to fulfill someone else's wishes instead of my own." There were self-pitying tears in his voice when he continued. "I'm a right mess, I am, Paisley Sterling. A right mess."

"Look, Huntley, let's get you something to eat and maybe some coffee…"

"Ha! Coffee won't help me now. But I'll tell you something that will help you and especially that uppity little lily-white sheila of yours."

"Now just a darn…"

"Stay away from Simmons," he whispered urgently. "Stay far away and maybe you'll come out of this alright."

"But…"

"And keep your nose out of something that happened so long ago it should have been forgotten."

Having said that, he lurched up from the booth and out of the restaurant. By the time I paid the bill for my uneaten lunch and followed him to the parking lot, his big white SUV was gone.

"Well, how do you like them apples?" I asked a fearless beady-eyed seagull who was perched on the post by my car.

CHAPTER TWENTY-EIGHT

No matter how hard I tried, I couldn't convince Cassie to eat out with me at the Dairy Queen—not even for the "healthy" side of the menu."

"A person can gain weight from just breathing in that place, Mom. You should really have gotten that out of your system by now. My, goodness, I feel like I'm dealing with a four year-old sometimes."

"Wow, you really know how to hurt a person," I teased.

"It's true and you know it."

"Well, maybe, but it is the only game in town, and I don't feel like driving down to Sallie's; and Gran's kitchen is so clean and all—it would be a real shame to go and dirty up the counters or any of the dishes that took so long to wash."

"Didn't you eat lunch down at the lake? Fish, I thought? That's what your note said, anyway."

"Yeah, well…you might as well know."

She turned around, her long shining hair swirling around her lovely face. "What? Know what?"

"My super-duper, eco-friendly, low-cal lunch was disturbed by your ex-boyfriend, the suspected drug dealer."

"Huntley? Huntley's still in town? Wow, I don't believe it."

"Well, he's here—and here to stay. He's bought part ownership in a little seafood restaurant near Minton on the lake, and I guess he plans to live there permanently."

"Minton, hmmm. Well, that's far enough away…"

"He looked awful, Cassie."

She sat down heavily on the kitchen chair—concern evident on her face.

"He's been on a bender. I'm almost positive. And he's lost weight. I thought he was ill, but he denied it. Said something about living a wasted life."

"Poor guy," she mused.

"Well, the poor guy seems to have it in for us—you in particular, and he warned us to stay away from William in no uncertain terms."

"That's odd."

"I thought so too. I mean, how would he even know William?"

"I guess I could ask him Saturday night."

"You're still going out with him? After Huntley's warning and all?

"Mom! A warning from the likes of Huntley Haverstock…a warning from him not to see someone with William's credentials?"

"You mean good looks, don't' you, Cassie?"

She stalked off like I knew she would. I had perfected the ability to push everyone's buttons over the years, and I needed some time alone to think…preferably on a full stomach.

Heeding Cassie's advice about not breathing in calories, I ordered at the drive-in window and ate in my car. I had ordered the grilled chicken salad again in honor of my health conscious daughter, and found it somewhat cumbersome and unwieldy to handle behind the wheel of the little compact. Not for the first time did I miss Watson. The big green Jeep Cherokee had gone to a fiery grave, but it had been fun to drive, and had much more room inside for everything—including a fast food feast.

The days were getting shorter as late autumn approached, and the lights in surrounding businesses along that strip of highway began to pop on like lightening bugs. Across the street from the Dairy Queen was a yard ornament emporium. Just a Quonset hut, really—with concrete geese and gnomes and other assorted creatures captured in cold grey stone. Mother had purchased one or two years ago for the farm, but I had never really liked them. To me, they appeared paralyzed—frozen by some evil wizard in the midst of their frolicking.

I noticed they had a new section featuring wooden lawn furniture—swings, benches, and one lone windmill that served as a flowerbox. For some reason, the windmill held my attention—knocking on the door of my memory like a vacuum cleaner salesman desperate for a sale.

"Windmill," I muttered. "What is it about that silly windmill? Oh, my God! Windmill!" Huntley Haverstock is in the windmill!"

The cardboard salad bowl and all the bits and pieces I hadn't eaten went flying to the floor when I jerked the car out of the parking lot and down the road towards home. There was a movie I had to see, and pronto.

Foreign Correspondent was there on the library shelf along with *Only Angels Have Wings, Without Reservations*, and all my other very favorite movies. It had been a long time since I had indulged in a night of popcorn and the old black and whites, but I remembered it took a few minutes into the movie before reporter Joel McCrea, and Harry Davenport, as his editor, agree upon a *nom de plume* for McCrea's character, Johnny Jones. But there it was: 'Huntley Haverstock'—big as you please!

What in the world, I wondered, had caused our little friend—no pun intended—to choose the name of that character—a hero no less—sent to another country to secure secrets about an impending war? I had always been a little bit infatuated with "Johnny Jones" and it didn't sit well with me to have his fake name besmirched by the likes of our "Huntley."

I had to find out who he really was, and pronto!

But first, I had to finish the movie. I particularly loved the thrilling part where Joel/Johnny/Huntley's trench coat sleeve gets caught in the gears of the big Dutch windmill and he nearly gets caught by the Nazi spy.

"Wow!"

CHAPTER TWENTY-NINE

The State Veterinary Board wouldn't budge. Privileged information they said—not for the public.

"Rats!"

Not to be undone before I even started, I called a friend at the Experiment Station outside of town. The University of Kentucky Research Center employed most of the Ph.D.'s in western Kentucky. I had made friends with several of them, and Jerry was one of the best.

"How's the serpent dog?" he chuckled. "Need any info on rabies?"

"No, Jerry, not yet—but there's still time. She's young."

I could see him sitting in his big messy lab surrounded by dogs and cats of all sizes and breeds—happy as could be—following his bliss.

"Still love the job, Jerry?"

"Oh, you know!" he laughed. "How can I help you, Paisley?"

"I need to know the names of any recent additions to the roster of vets in the state."

"You mean recent graduates?"

"No…I don't think so, just recent additions from out of state or even out of the country—say, Great Britain for example."

"Sounds like you already have someone in mind. What are you up to, Paisley, pet?"

"Nothing, really," I lied."

"You know this information is not for …"

"I know, I know—the public, yada yada yada." I decided to use Cassie. It wouldn't be the first time. "Let's just say a concerned mother wants to know about her daughter's new friend." Huntley was right. I was beginning to prove his assessment of me in spades.

I could practically see Jerry smile over the phone. He had three daughters himself, and was as protective as a papa bear.

"Well, in that case…hang on a minute."

I sat there holding my breath—wondering what Huntley was really up to—while Jerry fiddled around with his computer. He always acted like it was a complicated machine way beyond his comprehension, but I knew otherwise. He was a genius, plain and simple."

"Okay, Paisley? You still there?"

"Yep! Fire away."

"Last year, or this year? Or both?"

"Is it a long list? Somehow, I wouldn't think so."

"You'd be surprised. Lots of docs come here from other countries for further training in specialties that aren't offered in their countries. And some come for research at the Station."

"How about this year, then."

"Robert Timothy Andrew Alesworthy, Pierre Andres Benoit…"

"Wait a minute!" I couldn't believe my ears." Alesworthy?"

"Yep. Robert Timothy Andrew, no less."

"Where from? I mean where did he come from? Great Britain?"

"Well, in a manner of speaking. He comes from Australia. Has a pretty little bunch of degrees from the University of Melbourne, as a matter of fact. Smart lad."

I was astounded. I sat there thinking and then just to be sure, I asked, "Any Haverstocks on that list for the last two years?"

He was quiet for a moment and then told me that there was no Haverstock listed within the last four years.

"Sorry," he added. "Guess I couldn't be of much help."

"Oh, you'll never know, Jerry! Thanks a bunch."

I sat back in the kitchen chair and breathed deeply. No way could I have ever suspected that Huntley was Jane Alesworthy's son. It was downright unbelievable! That must be why he came back to Rowan Springs—to see his mother. But how had he ended up in Australia in the first place? I was practically bursting with questions when Cassie came home and found me lying on my stomach on the library floor with a big piece of poster board and a handful of markers making an outline of characters in our little melodrama.

"Oh, is it activity hour at the Meadowdale Nursery School?"

"No, smarty—it's show and tell. Sit down here on the floor and I'll show you and then you can tell me what you think."

CHAPTER THIRTY

Cassie was as astounded as I was. And she had even more questions.

"That little worm! What in the world is he up to?"

"My thoughts exactly!"

Aggie was delighted to have her mistress back home, and even more delighted that she was down on her level. She tugged and pulled on Cassie's jacket until Cassie gave in and played with her for a few minutes. But when she grabbed a red marker in her mouth and went running, I shouted something obscene and Cassie jumped up to catch her before any damage was done. Aggie and a red marker spelled trouble in any language.

Cassie came back, her cheeks only slightly less red than the dog's from her exertions. She held up the remnants of a chewed up red mess dripping with doggie spit.

"You don't want it back, I suppose?" she asked. "I'm really sorry, Mom. She wouldn't let it go."

Aggie followed behind her, looking as chastened as she ever got—her little black lips ringed with bright red ink. I couldn't help it. I laughed until I was hurting. The dog gave me her frostiest stare and left the room in a huff—headed no doubt, for my bed and whichever down pillow was her favorite of the moment.

"That red stuff better not come off on my pillows!"

"No, Mom. It's a permanent marker. It won't even come off my dog."

That was even funnier. This time it was my daughter who gave the frosty look and huffed out of the room, leaving me all by myself with the ever increasing mystery *du jour*.

It was late—way past library closing time, besides I didn't need their records when I had my own computer. I decided to google 'Huntley,' 'Jane Alesworthy,' and any other names I could think of that might shed some light on things. It wasn't until I got to 'James Arthur Poole' that I hit gold.

It was just a small paragraph in the Weiuca Weekly obituary section—not much to show for a long life. But James Arthur was deceased—had been for six months. He died at home in The Sunset Trailer Park. He lived alone as well—a widower—no mention of any progeny. He was found by a neighbor who checked in on him from time to time to make sure he was taking his heart medication. James was a double amputee—diabetes.

"Hmmm."

I fervently wished that Horatio wasn't having so much fun in the sun with my mother. There was no one else I could mull this new information over with. Andy was out of the question. He had already warned me off in no uncertain terms, and Cassie was mad at me because I laughed at her dog; but wasn't she always begging to get in on my snooping and sneaking around? Wasn't she the one who wanted so much to be included as a partner in crime?

Now, I decided, was the time to test her—to see if her desire to be number one son to my Charlie Chan—Tonto to my Lone Ranger—Cato to my Green Lantern…

"Not until you apologize for laughing at poor little Aggie," she protested.

"That's just plain childish! You can't have it both ways, baby. Either you're grown up enough to help me or you're not."

She pursed her pretty lips and then stuck out her tongue at me to make her point, and finally agreed.

"Ok, but do try not to make fun of Aggie in the future. She's sensitive, and …"

I couldn't help it. Not for love nor money could I hold it back. The great loud bark of a laugh startled even me.

CHAPTER THIRTY-ONE

Apparently Cassie's desire to become my part-time partner didn't run that deep. Once again, I was treated to two backsides—one slender and lovely and one fuzzy and white.

"Congratulations, old girl," I muttered. "You've done it again." Only this time I put more of the blame on Cassie. She was really acting out on an adolescent scale, but I decided it had more to do with her not wanting me to comment further on her Saturday date than anything else.

I considered 'Huntley's' warning again and found that I believed he was serious, and maybe more than just a little worried. Maybe his crush on my daughter had been real and he *was* concerned for her well being—in which case, it was time for me to become concerned as well.

William seemed innocent enough—made a little too perfect, but innocent. Meaning, I had found nothing on the Internet to cause any misgivings. It had been easy to find his background information—where he went to school, his graduate degree, his career thus far. He was an open book, or so I had thought. And his sister certainly had nothing to hide. She was so naïve and eager to please—she had practically told me her whole life story the other night after dinner.

Why, then, would Huntley, or Timothy, be so adamant that we stay away from him? Maybe tomorrow I could go back to the lake—to the little hamlet of Minton—and search him out. Surely his friend—the brand new owner of the little restaurant—would tell me where he was, or…

"Rats!"

How could I be so stupid? How in the world could I have overlooked the fact that Jane Alesworthy was Huntley's mother. She could quite obviously be the one who held the key to this whole mess. Maybe she wasn't as crazy as she had first appeared.

I tried to remember what she had said—something about receiving "lovely money" at one time. And she had called the murdered children "poor mites," and said that someone named "Meg" had known what happened but didn't tell. On one of her more lucid days, Jane might be able to testify in court, but who knew what she really knew?

I ruminated further, and my visit to the mental hospital began to take on a more sinister aspect. I was slowly coming to the conclusion that someone might have slipped the Queen a 'mickey,' as Leonard would say—a sleeping pill—before our little interview.

And it could even have been one of her regular meds—not something meant to stop her from talking. I needn't look for a murderer under every bush, like Horatio had warned me; but I had the uneasy feeling that if I were allowed to see her again the results would be the same.

Leonard always complained that a good detective had a perpetual headache from butting his head against a brick wall. First thing tomorrow, I decided, would be the time to check out his theory. Besides I hated being dependent on anyone else for information. That was the reason Andy Joiner and his fellow lawmen had so many reasons for disliking my methods—I was always in the way of their investigations. But now was not the time to be hesitant. Billy was in jail awaiting trial for a crime he did not commit and no one believed him but me—and maybe the absent Horatio.

"Enjoy your holiday, Horatio. And up and at 'em, Leonard," I muttered.

CHAPTER THIRTY-TWO

The beautiful Indian summer days appeared to have ended. Temperatures had dropped and the wind and rain made driving a nightmare as I resolutely headed back to Minton. I had to stop twice on the shoulder of the road because it was raining so hard I couldn't see. When I finally arrived I was exhausted and practically shaking from the stress.

Aside from my real reason for the trip, I now was really looking forward to a hot cup of coffee and maybe something to eat, but when I pulled up in front of the café there was a big "closed for remodeling" sign on the front door.

"Drat! Drat on every level!"

Somewhere in the little kid's part of my mind I could hear my mother saying, "You should have called first, dear." But that had never crossed my mind. Silly me.

I pulled my raincoat over my head and jumped out of the car and right into a huge puddle of standing water. Soaked up to my knees, I decided it couldn't get any worse and sloshed through the mud and gravel of the parking lot to the front door.

The rain had washed away most of the writing on the sign— certainly all the important information like the owner's name and phone number—but the new 'grand opening' date was clearly visible and just as clearly not worth anything to me because it was six months away.

I huddled under the sparse protection of the overhanging roof while I surveyed the rest of the street. Most of the other businesses were closed as well. The little towns around the lake depended on the summer tourists for their survival and closed down in the winter months while their owners tried to make a living doing something else. Minton was apparently such a place.

I was too dispirited to try anything more, but Leonard, or my own stupid pride, prodded me to ask at the gas station so I got back in the car and headed in that direction. As soon as I pulled under the portico, a man came running out the door and locked it behind him. He stopped for a moment and turned around when I hailed him, but shook his head and ran to a beat up old pickup and took off like a scared rabbit down the road.

"Well, I sure know how to clear the room," I grumbled. And then I heard the siren.

The little hairs on the back of my neck stood at complete attention and all the spit dried up in my mouth. I quickly turned on the radio and heard the tinny mechanical computer voice telling me to seek cover immediately.

The gas station attendant obviously didn't consider the meager roof of the station to be safe cover so, I imagined, neither must I. He was probably headed for his home and a nice safe basement stocked with all kinds of emergency supplies like flashlights and weather radios and nice hot coffee. Poor little me, on the other hand was far from home and had nothing but a very small car and a raincoat.

Mother and I had been through a tornado once before and it had unnerved me for weeks afterwards. I didn't relish going through that again, so I did a very stupid thing and turned around and decided to outrun it.

Fortunately, the State Patrol stopped me two miles on the other side of town. They stated the obvious when they told me my little compact was no protection against a storm the likes of which was headed our way. And they insisted that I follow them to the local high school where half the town and a few unwary travelers were being held.

Feeling like I was being escorted to prison, I followed the trooper reluctantly into the gym. I'm not sure what I expected—maybe hard grey cots and a few port-a-pottys—and if we were lucky, a table with bags of chips and stale cookies; but the huge room was warm and surprisingly cozy with tables and chairs and a buffet of hot food.

"Coffee's over there, miss, if you want some," stated the trooper, "and the ladies accommodations are behind that portable wall in the middle of the gym." He tipped his hat and added pointedly, "You'll be safer here than on the road. Just make sure you stay until the danger's over. Makes my job a lot easier."

Feeling chagrined and suitably chastened, I made my way over to the coffee table and thanked the nice lady when she gave me two cardboard cups of great smelling coffee.

"They're small, honey. I'd give you three but you only got two hands," she giggled. "Come back for more and some cookies when you've warmed up and dried off a bit."

CHAPTER THIRTY-THREE

Worn out by the harried drive and warmed by the surprisingly good coffee and delicious chocolate chip brownie, I lay down on one of the cots set up in the women's section and dozed off. I must not have slept that deeply because somewhere in the background of many muted conversations I heard the unmistakable sound of a voice as Australian as a didgeridoo.

"Huntley!" I shouted as I sat up, wide awake. The few women around me looked over curiously but soon decided I was having a nightmare and turned back to their card games and laptops.

I shrugged off my wrinkled raincoat and ran my fingers through impossibly tangled red curls. I knew I must look like a scarecrow, but that didn't matter right now. I had to find Huntley. Getting up stiffly from the cot I peered around the partition and searched the crowd in the auditorium. Most of the men were huddled around one side of the hot food buffet—drawn to it no doubt because of the price—free, and the charming looks of the three nubile young women serving.

Listening carefully for the accent of the bush, I walked slowly through the gym. I heard snatches of conversations about this and that—mostly concerns over pets left behind—and worry about crops and cattle. One woman was having a quiet come apart in the corner, and I almost went over to see if I could help. Thankfully, I was too slow in acting on my feelings of compassion and a young man she obviously knew came over and put his arms around her. When she stopped crying and looked up at him with love in her eyes I almost teared up a bit; but realizing it was mostly feelings brought on by my own fear and exhaustion, I shrugged it off and continued my search.

"Here ya are, mate, have a bit of this right tucker and she'll be apples in no time."

I turned around and saw a small boy at the other end of the buffet holding out his plate while a big rangy dark- bearded man filled it to the brim. "Don't go walkabout and forget the chokkie, now."

The little boy grinned back. "Too right! Mr. Mick!"

'Mr. Mick' was still chuckling when I approached. He looked me up and down and whistled.

Well, I'll be gobsmacked! Where did you come from, lass? A bit of lippy and you'd be right spiff!"

"Thank you, I think."

"Some hot tucker, gorgeous? Good for what ails ya." His smile was a fifty-watter at least, and I found myself warming to Mick instantly—but business was business.

"Huntley. I need to know about your friend Huntley…or Timothy Alesworthy, or whatever he is calling himself at the moment."

The smile disappeared like the sun going behind clouds. His eyes darkened and his answer was terse.

"I'm no dobber."

"Pardon?"

"Look, I'm a busy as a cat burying shit, so if you don't mind…"

"Just tell me where he is?"

"You can go on with your ear bashing all you want. Like I said, I'll not dob on any bloke."

I turned away and looked for a place to sit down where I could keep Mr. Down Under in my sight the rest of the afternoon. A nice little cot pulled back against the wall was comfortable enough, and I settled in for my surveillance.

People came and went—Mick loading up plate after plate with a smile and a kind word for everyone. Either he was a genuinely nice man or he was a shoo-in for the Australian Oscar.

Finally a pretty young thing hurried over to take his place. She reached up and gave him a quick peck on the cheek and took over his apron. They both shared a laugh because it hung way down below her knees. He gave her a cheeky salute and walked away from the table and away from me.

I went running.

CHAPTER THIRTY-FOUR

I called after Mick but couldn't tell if he was ignoring me, or just couldn't hear above the roar of the crowd in the auditorium. It seemed in the last few minutes that the throng had doubled. Most of the new arrivals appeared to be emergency workers from the look of the bright orange jackets and hard hats. And they all were headed straight for the food. I felt like a salmon swimming upstream against the tide of tired, but hungry folks who had done a job above and beyond and were poised to head back out in the wind and rain as soon as they had something warm and filling to eat and drink.

For a moment I felt selfish and frivolous—all these people were helping a community in peril, and I was probably just wasting my time and theirs with a fool's errand, But then I thought about Billy huddled in his cell waiting for news of the reprieve I had promised him, and I pushed onwards.

I finally caught up to Mick right outside of the men's bathroom. He turned around and winked at me and went straight inside. Without any thought of my mother's southern lady manners, or my own sensibilities, I followed.

"Wow! You are a gutsy little sheila!" he laughed. "I'll give you that!"

"I just wanted to make sure you know I'm serious about talking to you. And—that there are no other windows or doors in here."

"Too right, love. I'll be right out, I promise."

"We all promise," came a chorus of at least three other voices behind closed stalls.

Mick burst out laughing, and I could feel my face going up in flames. I quickly backed up to the door, turned around and blindly fought my way outside. I could never remember being so horribly embarrassed.

When Mick came out, rubbing his hands together to get them dry he was still laughing. He laughed even harder when I pleaded with him not to disclose what had just happened.

"I mean, I don't really know you …well, not at all, but if my mother ever found out…"

"Don't worry. Settle down, lass and let's take a load off over here in the corner. Seems like I've been on my feet for hours… actually, I have been on my feet for hours. Damn tornado!"

"Too right!" I grinned back. I don't know what I expected, and I hoped with all my heart that he wouldn't disappoint me, but Mick seemed to be one of the good guys.

"Are you really from Australia, or is all that bonzer talk straight out of some *Crocodile Dundee* movie?"

It was Mick's turn to blush a shade or two of crimson. "Just between you and me, miss, I do put on a bit of a show now and again, but it's good for business, or it's gonna be when I open up the café."

"So what *is* your connection to down under? And Huntley, or Timothy?"

"Andrew."

"Who?"

"Andrew Alesworthy. That's what my Aunt Jane always called him, anyway."

"Queen Jane is your aunt?" I was floored.

"So you've met the dear old soul, have ya?"

"Yes, I have, and you are right. She is a dear, but what's going on here between you and Tim…Andrew, and Jane."

He took in a big breath and sighed. He was tired from a long hard day, and I began to feel badly about ambushing him at the end of it. But as long as he was willing to talk, I wanted to listen.

"Andrew is my cousin…one I'd never actually met until recently, mind you. The oldies—my parents—that is, migrated to the US when I was just a babe. Dad came over here on a job and Ma liked it so much—the trees and lakes were so different from the dry back home, they decided to stay. Dad's older sister—that's Aunt Jane—followed shortly afterwards when her fiancé died in a freak accident—and she finished her education degree.

"But where does Andrew come in?"

"Gettin' to that in a minute. A friend of Jane's got in a spot of trouble awhile back and wanted a change of scenery, so to speak. Auntie told her about her family in Melbourne and said they'd be glad to take her in—so she went. Didn't take her long to fall for my Uncle Roger and the next thing you know—along comes Andrew."

"So he really is Australian, not British."

"Where'd you get that idea? Of course not! Andrew may be a lot of things, but he's no bloody whinging Pom!"

CHAPTER THIRTY-FIVE

I went and got us some more coffee and some cookies, but after a while even that couldn't keep Mick from slurring his words from exhaustion. I decided to take pity on him and let him stretch for "a bit of nappy."

I was long past caring if he really knew the vernacular or was making it up as he went along. He made it sound real enough, and he certainly looked the part. I found myself hoping he would succeed in his 'shrimp on the Barbie' business, and looked forward to partaking of it with maybe Cassie and the Raleighs in tow.

I went back to my cot, but someone had already settled in—using my wadded up raincoat as a pillow—so I sought the solitude of the far end of the gym and found an empty space complete with a fresh clean pillow and a nice warm blanket. I was asleep in minutes.

When I woke up again, the gym was almost empty. I couldn't believe I had slept through the night—through all the hustle and bustle and activity—and the all-clear.

The food line was still there, but the pickings were poor. I grabbed a couple of pieces of burnt toast and a slice of cheese. Another cup of the more-than-decent coffee, and I had my breakfast at a table where I could watch for Mick.

I was on my second cup when I decided that he had most likely left earlier in the morning when the all-clear had sounded. It was time for me to go home, too.

After a desultory search for my raincoat, I slogged my way through the parking lot and found my pitiful little car covered with branches and flyaway garbage from the nearby dumpster. It took a good twenty minutes to clean enough mud and refuse off so I could safely drive, and another twenty minutes trying to get out of the parking lot, which was also covered with garbage and branches.

When I finally got to a clear space, I had to wait for a line of emergency vehicles to get back on the road. It was slow going all the way and I was worn out when I finally arrived at Meadowdale Farm.

Cassie ran out to meet me.

"Mom! I was so worried! Why didn't you call, or answer my calls? You would have killed me if I had gone off the grid like that."

"I know, honey, I know, but the cell towers were down and only the police and firemen could use what landlines there were and…"

She launched herself at me and gave me a great big hug. She smelled sweet and clean and reminded me how stinky and dirty I had to be.

She must have known it, too.

"You go and have a nice hot shower and I'll fix you a great big farm breakfast—just like you like it—bacon and eggs and…"

"Cassie, baby, if you don't mind, I think I'll have the shower and skip the food. All I want is my own wonderful soft bed. The drive back was a bear, and I'm pooped. How about a nice hot dinner instead?"

And so we enjoyed some delicious eggs Benedict with a fresh spinach salad in front of the fire that evening while I regaled Cassie with Mick stories.

"He does sound like a trip," Cassie said.

"A very entertaining fellow, I must admit."

"But the men's bathroom. Mom! I can't believe…"

"Now, remember you promised never to tell anyone about that."

"Pinky swear," she chuckled. "But wouldn't Gran just…"

"Pinky swear, Cass," I warned.

"So where does the money come from, you think?"

"What money?" For a minute I was confounded. Had I missed something?

"The money Huntley, or Andrew is using to finance Mick's shrimp place, of course?"

"Damn! You right. How in the world did I miss that?"

"Gosh, maybe I am your partner in crime after all!" She smiled. "And don't forget," she continued after a moment, "your Ph.D. friend said Andrew had several degrees from the University of Melbourne. Higher learning doesn't come cheap."

"You right about that, too, Cassie. Way to go, partner."

CHAPTER THIRTY-SIX

Amazingly enough, I slept through the night again—without any tornado induced nightmares. Seems I might be getting used to the little devils. And from the look around the farm on what had turned out to be one of those beautiful clear autumn days—bright sunshine and lovely blue skies—no bad weather had come our way.

"I watched the radar on the weather channel the whole time you were missing, Mom. It was real scary but very localized. Just the land between the lakes and the little towns surrounding were the only ones affected."

"Lucky me."

"Very lucky you! And don't you forget it. That makes two near misses now, doesn't it?"

"Mmfff."

"Good breakfast?"

"Yummy!"

"Celedia did emphasize the art of making an arepa."

"Delicious, honey. I'd forgotten how good they are. And this white Mexican cheese from Morgantown was definitely worth the trip. I reached for another little hot South American corn cake and slathered on the butter.

"Too bad butter is so bad for you," she admonished.

"Now don't you start, missy. Best breakfast I've had in years, and I want to enjoy it without any guilt."

"Really, Mom—the best?"

Cassie floated out of the kitchen on a cloud of pride while I cleaned up. I was in such a great mood—with my satisfied tummy and my joy in being home unscathed—it took washing a whole sink full of dishes before I realized this was the day. Cassie's date with William the Weird was tonight—unless I could derail it some-how.

"But think how much fun it will be! We haven't gone shopping together in ages, and we could stay in one of those big fancy hotels near the mall and just spend money to our heart's content. And eat…we could eat anywhere you want…even that vegetarian place you've always wanted to take me to."

"Well…"

"Come on Cassie! Gran and Horatio won't be back until next weekend and it's really kinda lonely here without her to bitch at me about something. Say 'yes'—please?"

"What about Aggie?"

"Well…we could try that new doggie farm they've been advertising in the paper. 'You leave 'em—we love 'em.'"

"Yes, but Aggie's got specials needs."

"Ha! It's high time she got over 'her special needs.'"

"You're losing me, Mom. Besides, I don't want to break my date with William at the last minute. That's really bad form and even you have to admit it's rude."

"Well…yeah, but clothes, Cassie…and shoes. Don't forget shoes."

"I have an idea. We could leave early tomorrow morning. We would still have almost a week to shop and play. I'll make reservations now. How about that new Hilton Inn Suites behind the mall?"

And she turned around to her computer and left me to wander out of her room like a zombie. How in the world did I ever get myself in such a mess? Cassie's South American grandfather used to quote an old saying about losing the goat *and* the rope. Looks like I had done just that.

CHAPTER THIRTY-SEVEN

I spent the rest of the afternoon working half-heartedly on my 'cast of characters.' The big piece of poster board I had been using was almost full of names and notes and looked very colorful even without the red marker.

I propped the cardboard up on the hearth and sat back against the sofa to take it all in. Several things began to stand out—and lots more questions appeared unanswered.

For example: why had Jane been living in the house on Market Street instead of with her brother's family in Minton? When a possible answer occurred to me I jumped up and turned on my computer to search the teacher rosters in Rowan Springs at the time. Sure enough, Mary Jane Alesworthy taught world history to the high school students at Saint Anthony's for three years during the same time Eliza and Abigail Poole were students in lower school. Jane could well have been one of the teachers mentioned in the newspaper article. She would have known the children from living in the same house and most likely would have spoken to their father about their illnesses.

Maybe she was even having an affair with James Poole instead of the live-in housekeeper. No, I decided—she was recovering from losing her fiancé in an accident. Romance was probably the last thing on her mind. And speaking of the housekeeper—who was Margaret and where had she gone?

I couldn't remember if I had gotten to Margaret's name when I was perusing the Internet the other night. I did seem to remember stopping when I found James Poole's obituary. Maybe one of my little search engines could find Margaret Nance Whitelaw.

It was only a small paragraph—really only an afterthought in an article written by a reporter over a decade ago. It was listed as an unsolved mystery—a 'cold case' from the past that intrigued him. He wrote that someday he would like to refer to the case in a novel about 'ladies of mystery.' Margaret Whitelaw was acquitted of murdering two children in 1954. Since then she had eluded all efforts to locate her. According to the writer, the case was never solved. Someone got away with murder.

Where, indeed, had Margaret gone?

There was something else I had forgotten. I had never looked up the name of the police chief at the time. I could call Andy Joiner and ask him for the official records but I was positive he would refuse. And what in the world made him warn me off this business in the first place. All the principals in my little cast of characters—with the exception of mad Queen Jane and Andrew were dead—who was left to cause mayhem?

When the smell of overheated cardboard hit my nose, I snatched the poster away from the hearth and lay it on the coffee table to cool off. I swapped places and sat down in front of the fire to warm my back. The evenings were getting chilly and we had not turned on the furnace yet. The fire felt good.

"Wow! It's burning up in here," noted Cassie as she breezed in looking too good for her own good in camel slacks and turtleneck sweater to match. "And it smells funny—like something's burning."

"Well, it's not, and I'm cold," I grumbled.

"I'm all packed," she announced gaily. "Didn't take long. I left a lot of room in my suitcase for all the new duds you promised me. You ready for our trip?" she asked, checking her hair and makeup in the mirror.

"I will be by the time you get back. What time did you say that was, anyway?"

"Didn't say, Mother dearest," she answered pointedly.

"You said something about *Les Miserables?*"

"The show's over at eleven, but William mentioned something about a late dinner near Barkley Dam somewhere."

"Where…somewhere?"

"Don't know, and I'm a big girl now. I don't have to tell you where I am all the time. And you certainly didn't bother telling me where you spent the last thirty-six hours."

"Cassie, I told you what happened."

"Just sayin'…Oh, don't be such a worry wart. I'll text you and let you know when I find out myself. Okay?"

CHAPTER THIRTY-EIGHT

Wishing whole-heartedly that I had never ever said anything about a shopping spree in Atlanta, I got up from my warm spot in front of the fire and hunted out my suitcase. Inside there were still a few things from my last trip—socks, new underwear still in the plastic package, and my extra toiletries. Packing wasn't going to be so bad after all.

I messed around in the closet for a bit and finally decided on the usual jeans and sweaters. Maybe, I thought, I should replenish my wardrobe as well. But then where did I ever go to show off new clothes? And what did I really need. The answer was nothing. So I took out the few things I had in the big suitcase and put them in a small carryall. I added a new Michael Connelly paperback for those nights when Cassie was sure to visit friends from Emory, and I was done.

Grabbing a quick bite from the kitchen, I headed back to the library for some more Internet sleuthing. For a moment it struck me as strange that Aggie had not been dancing around me while I fixed my ham sandwich. She usually begged for a tidbit whenever the refrigerator door opened. When I entered the library I found out why.

She lay on the floor in a puddle of brightly colored doggie vomit—panting heavily, and covered from head to toe in blue, green, yellow and orange marker ink.

My first instinct was to call out for Cassie, but she wasn't here. She wasn't here, and I had no idea where she was or when she would return. Aggie was my problem, and I had better do all the right things—and fast.

Picking her up gently, I saw right away that she didn't even have the strength to growl—much less bite me. And that was bad—really bad. Her little black lips were pale and her tongue was dry. From the quick look I had gotten of what she had thrown up and what was missing from the box, she had to have ingested three—maybe four markers. Her heartbeat was slow and heavy and her little chest barely moved when she took quick shallow breaths.

The dog was dying. And it would be my fault. I did the only thing I could think of—I wrapped her in a big fluffy towel and got in the car and headed for the vet's office as fast as I could go.

Doctor White had returned from vacation. I had seen that in the newspaper last week. I hoped and prayed that he was keeping late hours, because both Lanierville and Morgantown were too far away. From the deteriorating look of her condition, Aggie would be dead long before I could get to another vet in either town.

The lights were out when I pulled up in front of the animal hospital. I honked the horn a few times and then got out and banged on the door—in frustration more than anything. When a light went on somewhere in the back of the building I almost wept with relief. I grabbed Aggie's barely warm little body from the car, and burst inside when the door opened. I almost dropped her along with my jaw when I saw who opened it.

"Why, what brings you here, Paisley love?" asked none other than Huntley Haverstock in the flesh. "Ah, looks like Cassie's deadly little dingo is in big trouble."

But from that moment, Huntley/Andrew was all business. He gently lifted the dog from my arms and ran back to the surgery with her. I thought he would object to my following, but he started asking for things immediately.

I did the best I could. Stumbling around the unfamiliar surgery, I fetched tubes and needles and things I didn't even want to know the names of—or how they were to be used. For two hours or more, Andrew worked feverishly—and expertly—to save Aggie's life. When he had done all he could do—when she was cleaned out and hooked up to a saline solution and something else to help steady her heart rate, he sat back on his stool and looked up at me.

"I think she's going to make it."

"She'd damn well better make it, you crazy little Aussie!"

And with that I slid down on the cold floor and cried my eyes out.

CHAPTER THIRTY-NINE

"I deserved that," He admitted. "Well, maybe not just right now. I did a really good job of saving that miserable little beastie's life, you have to admit. But I did deserve that for all the trouble I've caused you and Cassie."

"I do, and you did," I wailed.

He came around the surgery table where Aggie lay breathing peacefully and gave me a hand up off the floor. "What's say me and you go put on the tucker-bag? Eh?"

"What?" I snuffled.

"Supper. I'm starving after that little act of heroics and you look a bit down in the mouth yourself. There's a place down the road. I've gotten quite attached to it since I came here. It's called the Dairy Queen. Maybe you're familiar…"

I laughed. "You bet! But what about Aggie? We can't leave her here by herself. What if she wakes up and rolls off the table—or has a relapse?"

"Don't worry. John, Doctor White's assistant, had an early date tonight which is why I was still in the office when you came. He'll be here any minute now, and I'll make sure he knows to keep a close eye out for any change in her condition. We won't be far away—couple of blocks really—and I'll check back to see how she is before I go home tonight."

I was too tired to argue, so when the young man arrived, I listened with half an ear while Andrew filled him in on the treatment Aggie had received and the things to look for if she were to get sicker. As we walked towards the front door, I handed him my car keys.

"You mind driving? I'll feel better after we eat, but right now I don't trust myself."

"Sure, if you have any petrol left," he said, cocking his head toward my compact.

And as he spoke the car—whose engine I had left on in my haste to get help for Aggie, sputtered and died."

"Drat!"

"So we'll go in mine."

It went against all my instincts—of all the things I had warned Cassie about—'don't get in a stranger's car' ranked number one. But I was tired and hungry, and honestly didn't know what else to do. Everyone important to me was out of pocket at the moment. Surely the man who just saved my dog's life wouldn't turn around and endanger mine.

I gave him a wan smile and waited while he brought his Land Rover from the back of the building. Shutting down all the primitive centers in my brain that fired away when danger was near—when the pterodactyl hovered overhead, or the saber-toothed tiger was on the prowl—I climbed into Andrew's SUV and headed blithely towards my other major nemesis—the infamous Dairy Queen.

It was almost closing time, but since we were both apparently very good customers, they let us come inside; and while they mopped and cleaned, we ate cheeseburgers and fries without any trepidation whatsoever.

Neither of us spoke until the last bit of ketchup had been swabbed up by the last fry, and then we both started at once.

"How did you…?" I began.

"It's time I came…" said he.

We both laughed—exhaustion heavy in our voices. I motioned for him to continue.

"Can I trust you, Paisley? I mean I did just work my butt off to save your little dingo's hide. Some would say you owe me."

I thought for a moment. I wasn't quite sure I trusted Andrew, but I did know that come what may—I could always be counted on for doing the right thing whatever that was. I told him so.

"Then I guess that'll have to do. After all, I've done nothing wrong—to anyone but myself. And I've screwed that up royally."

"What?"

"My life. I wasted my whole life trying to live for someone else—trying to get revenge for someone else."

"Who, Andrew? Who have you been ruining your life for?"

He looked at me for a moment and then out into the night. I saw ghosts fleeting in his eyes. I shivered and wrapped my arms around my shoulders. I felt as cold as his voice was when he spit out the answer.

"My mum. My poor sweet miserable deluded little mum."

CHAPTER FORTY

As much as they wanted our continued good business, we could tell the DQ was ready to say, "Nite, nite" to its best customers.

We helped clean off our table; grabbed "to go" cups, and headed back to Andrew's SUV. I was so tired I could barely climb inside. The night had gotten a bit chilly and Andrew turned on the heater without being asked.

"Guess you're not used to this cold weather?"

"Heater feels good," he mumbled. "Actually everything here is aces with me. Mainly because it's not "there" where she suffered so much unhappiness. Well, she did here too, but that was long ago, and seems another world."

"Tell me, Andrew. Tell me what you mean."

"The truth is, I was the one who suffered in Oz, and I'm just beginning to realize how much."

We had pulled up behind the animal hospital and sat there with the big engine running quietly enough to hear the sound of frogs and crickets in the adjoining field. I discovered I was a little surprised that I could hear them somewhere else besides the farm. And then Andrew dropped a real surprise in my lap.

"She never killed those two little nippers, you know. She was completely innocent."

"Margaret Whitelaw is your mother?"

"Meg Whitelaw was my mother. She's cactus now. Stone cold dead, and I hope she's finally found the peace that eluded her in life."

"Oh, Andrew, I'm so sorry."

He turned around and faced me with anger in his eyes. "How could you be sorry? You never even met her. Never even knew how fragile she was. How tormented. She was a wonderful lady, but she couldn't let go of the hate that consumed her. Not even after she married Dad and had me and a fine life—even if it was in the back of Bourke."

"Where?"

He hung his head, and I hear a little sniffle. I was astounded. Huntley Haverstock never cried. But poor Andrew did. I let him have a moment to pull himself together and then asked all my questions—the ones I had been boiling over with.

"So the 'back of Bourke' is a long way off—as in a long way from Melbourne?"

"Right you are."

"And you mother went to Oz—Australia—after…"

"After she was acquitted of two murders for lack of evidence," he spat out. "Two murders that someone else committed—someone she was too scared of to point the finger at."

"Is that someone still alive?"

"Not anymore!" he laughed grimly.

"Andrew, you didn't…?"

"Kill him? No I don't have it in me to kill anyone, apparently. A right coward, I am."

"Not a coward, I think. Not a coward at all. Maybe you just know the moral difference between right and wrong."

"Maybe," he mumbled. I could see he was getting tearful again.

As much as I was beginning to sympathize with young Andrew—Leonard was demanding answers.

"And maybe I just always knew she was a bit sick—sick in the head—sweet and wonderful, but messed up in a very bad way. And she did the wrong thing when she tried to make me over. Create an instrument of her vengeance—to make a weapon out of her only child to right all the wrongs done to her in the past."

He looked up, and I could see the vast sadness in his eyes. It was one of those moments we all have when we grow up and realize our parents are not invincible—not the paragons of virtue we always believed. That his whole life had been shaped by the wishes of a woman, who while not completely insane, was very, very flawed.

CHAPTER FORTY-ONE

"Let's go inside and get more comfortable," I suggested. "I have a feeling you have much more on your mind—much more you'd like to get off your chest."

He suddenly looked at me suspiciously. "I'm not going to be the bloke in your next novel, am I?"

"Considered it. Dropped it," I assured him. "I don't really speak your language. All that 'bloke' and 'dingo' and 'back of Bourke'— is way too complicated for me," I added with a smile.

"And I went to uni. You should hear my cousin, Mick. Now there's a right cobber!"

It slipped out before I thought, "I have, and you're right—if that means he's a nice guy."

"You what?"

"Um, met him. The other day during the tornado," I admitted, hoping that would be the end of it.

"Checking up on me, were you, Paisley Sterling? Trying to find out if I was fair dinkum?"

"Well, you did leave kind of a bad impression…"

"Lying about my name and all…?"

"And that's another thing -'Huntley Haverstock'? Where did you ever come up with that?"

"Favorite old movie of me mum's. She always did love Joel McCrea. Said her Roger looked just like him."

"Roger? As in Mick's Uncle Roger?"

"Right as rain."

Then your dad was your Aunt Janes's…"

"Older brother."

"So Jane and your mother…"

"Were friends…neighbors, really. They lived in a big old rooming house here in Rowan Springs. It's gone now. Torn down for a…"

"Quickie Mart," I filled in absently.

"You seem to know a lot," he noted.

I waved my hand back and forth. I was thinking furiously—hoping I wouldn't shut him up—make him turn tail and run; but I had to know the rest.

"So who was she afraid of? Who really killed Eliza and Abigail? Who was it that she so afraid of all these years?"

"Why, I'm surprised you haven't figured that out yet. Their dad, of course."

"That poor old diabetic double amputee who died in Weiuca City awhile back?"

"Poor old vicious pervert, you mean. My mum and Jane saw him abuse those little girls from day one. He even made them watch on some occasions. Quite enjoyed an audience, he did. Nasty bit of business, that."

"Oh, my," I gasped.

"Finally they got up some gumption and threatened to tell the authorities. But he said no one would believe a foreign woman or a woman who had the reputation Mum had gotten from living with him as a housekeeper. And he killed the girls slowly just to get the point across that he had all the power."

"His own daughters?"

"He was a monster, no two ways about it. He deserved to die, but I didn't have the guts to do it, Paisley. I'm a right mess, I am." He hung his head and swiped at his eyes.

"You've said that before, Andrew. I believed it then, but I don't now."

I reached over and patted him tentatively on the shoulder. I wasn't used to consoling anyone I wasn't related to, but I knew a soul in torment when I saw one.

CHAPTER FORTY-TWO

He looked up after a while, his eye suspiciously bright, "You know about Millicent Grazianni, too?" he asked.

I was startled. I'd quite forgotten about Millicent with everything else going on. "What about her?"

"She saw it, too."

"You mean the murders?"

"I mean everything. She was just a little girl then—younger than Eliza, but I'm sure they played together. It would have been strange had they not. Must have been quite disturbing to watch a playmate being used like that. It's too disturbing for me to think about even now, and I'm a grown man. Poor little thing."

He sniffed for a few more minutes while I waited for the rest of the story to come out.

"At first, Mum and Jane tried to get her to tell, you know? But she was too scared. They insisted her parents would believe her, if no one else. But I'm not so sure. That was a long time ago and people didn't speak of such things. And certainly not with a child. And her dad and mum depended on their tenants for a living. James Poole was probably right in his assertion that he was above reproach. That nobody would believe a fine upstanding citizen would do such a hideous thing."

"And so he killed his own daughters, and ruined three other young lives in the process."

"Rightly so. Jane went gradually mental, although I think she probably had a better life than the other two. Mum grew old and bitter—full of hate and the overwhelming desire for revenge, and Madame Grazianni started using herself for a carving board before her teens."

"I should have figured that out. Self-harmers are usually young women who are full of guilt. Horatio was right about that."

"I like him," added Andrew vaguely. "Nice old gent."

I pondered Andrew's 'confessions' for a moment. It was quiet in the office. The seats inside Doc White's personal domain were deep and soft—I found myself wishing I could curl up and just sleep for a thousand years. Maybe when I woke up, the world would be a better place—free of hate and misery—somewhere warm and cozy and…

"Paisley!"

"Uh?"

"You fell asleep for a minute. Let me take you home. Now that I've unloaded all my troubles on you, I feel like I could sleep like a babe, too. We can always talk again tomorrow."

"Mmfff. Couldn't I just sleep here?" I curled up even tighter to get more comfortable. "There's nobody to go home to…if I could just sleep until tomorrow morning early?"

Andrew laughed. "Early in this office is early indeed. Things start buzzing around four o'clock in the morning. By six you'll swear you've booked a stateroom on Noah's ark. And, if you don't mind my asking, where is everybody?"

"I know you mean 'where is Cassie?' so I'll just come right out and tell you, she's out on a date. And Mother and Horatio are in the Bahamas—just in case you did mean 'everybody.'"

"I fell a little bit in love with Cassie, you know?"

"Most everyone does at some point."

"Who's the victim this time?"

"A new guy—from out of town. William Simmons. He's the…"

"Crickey! Could things get any worse?"

"Worse? What's worse?"

"Cassie! Didn't Joiner tell you to not go all stickybeak on this?" He shook his head and jumped up, pacing the floor in short economic strides. "I simply cannot believe this! You let your precious daughter go out with that likes of that dunny rat!"

"Rat?"

"Dunny rat—it's a whole lot worse than a plain rat," he answered absently. "Where did they go?" he demanded.

"They went to see a play…a musical, really."

"In Weiuca City? Then they should be home by now. Let's go make sure."

He grabbed my hand and pulled me up from the warm soft nest I had made. "Come on," he practically shouted. "Hurry!"

I pulled my hand and arm back from his grasp. "They…they were going to grab a bite afterwards—somewhere near the dam. I'm…I'm not sure exactly where."

"Bloody hell!"

Thus time I had no trouble climbing in Andrew's big SUV—adrenaline fueled me all the way. I could feel it thrumming in my veins as we barreled along down the Interstate towards Barkley Lake and the dam. At Andrew's insistence, I had called Andy Joiner and told him Cassie was out with Simmons. I didn't even have to explain a thing. Andy was all over it—barking orders and summoning his troops while I waited nervously on hold.

I also didn't have time to ask Andrew what the hell was going on before Andy was back with instructions for me.

"Tell Alesworthy to take you home—and then stay there," he shouted. "Do not budge! Let us take care of things this time. Okay? Do I have an 'okay'?" he insisted.

"Yes, Andy," I answered, meekly. "Please find Cassie and protect her from whatever is going on," I begged.

"Of course, Paisley," he answered soothingly. "Of course, I will. Don't worry. And stay put!"

I turned around to Andrew and lied through my teeth. "He wants us to meet him at Barkley Dam." I was fairly certain he had heard both ends of the conversation. Andy had been loud enough. He knew I wasn't telling the truth, but he was also not in the mood to take me home and be late getting to the scene of the search. He stomped down on the gas pedal and we went racing into the night.

CHAPTER FORTY-THREE

I was bewildered. William had seemed innocent enough—even a bit boring, despite Cassie's insistence that he was a bit off-putting, a bit queer.

"You're thinking Simmons seems a too right bloke, even if he does have kangaroos loose in the paddock."

"Someday you'll have to teach me Australian," I complained. "But not now. And 'yes' he didn't set off in warning bells—at least in the few times I was around him."

"Well—I know for a fact that he's an extortionist, and Joiner suspects that he's a murderer. How's that for bell ringing?"

"Oh, my God! Cassie…!"

"Precisely!"

He had to slow down when we got to a hill behind two eighteen wheelers passing each other. He drummed his fingers on the steering wheel. His nervousness frightened me.

"When did you and Andy get to be such pals?" I asked to distract him so we wouldn't end up in a ditch.

"After that night on your front porch," he smiled—his face turning red then white from the reflection of the blinking lights on the back of the trucks. "Your little girl sure packs a wallop."

"Let's hope so," I answered fervently.

"I decided then and there I'd better make nice with the locals in case she lodged some kind of a complaint. I went to see Joiner and told him everything I know."

"Which you still haven't told me, by the way."

One truck finally pulled ahead of the other and Andrew sped around and took off trying to make up for lost time.

He took a deep breath, letting out as much stress as he could. "Jane was blackmailing the Grazianni woman from the moment she married that rich foreigner guy."

"Which much have been for the better part of thirty years!"

"Exactly. All my life."

"My God! She was sending you the money, wasn't she? For your education?"

"Not me, my mum. She didn't have much luck with husbands. Her first died after a year of marriage, and Dad died when I was just a nipper. She had no insurance money to fall back on and we were in a bad way. Jane came up with the nifty little idea of 'suggesting' to the new bride that she could help Mum out with my upbringing in return for their silence. Jane promised she and Meg would never tell about her part in the little basement vignettes on Market Street for Millicent's cooperation. Mum didn't tell me about where the money to take care of us was coming from until her last illness—about six months ago."

"But Millicent didn't do anything," I protested.

"Tell that to her. She felt as guilty as if she had done the dirty deeds. Deluded maybe, and certainly disturbed, but she was also afraid of Poole finding out that she might confess what she had seen and incriminate him. She was really scared. Jane promised to keep her safe."

"But she was in no position to do that!"

"I know and you know, but poor Millicent believed it. She paid out the wazoo for almost thirty years to a crazy little old lady for 'pretend' protection from a real live monster."

CHAPTER FORTY-FOUR

"So where does William come into this awful business?"

"Jane was careful at first. She sent the checks to her bank and had them forward almost everything to Australia, but as her dementia got worse she had to have help. She made the mistake of trusting the wrong person."

"William?"

"Too right! He started helping himself to a little cut of the moolah—just a bit at first, but then he got greedy and began taking more and more until my mum was left high and dry, and Jane got nothing at all—just room and board as long as she was useful."

We were almost at the dam now. I could see the dark water ahead and the long line of bright lights across the spillway gates.

"Did Jane confront him? Surely someone would have listened to her."

"Crazy little old lady complains about the director of the mental hospital taking money from her? I think not!"

"No," I shook my head sadly, "I guess not."

"But *he* did confront *her*."

I pointed to the lights of a restaurant up ahead and Andrew pulled into the parking lot. We drove around slowly looking for Cassie or William inside the brightly lit café.

"See anything?" I asked.

"Afraid not. What's up ahead?"

"The Pelican is the only other place I know that would still be open this late."

He nodded slowly, and then drove back around one more time to make sure before taking off.

"So you were saying…?" I asked just to keep from screaming with nervous tension. I was getting really, really scared about what might happen to Cassie if we didn't get to her in time.

"The money dried up. Jane just wasn't getting any more checks. By now William had gotten nervy enough to intercept them before they even reached her, so he knew for sure. She told me that he went to her room and threatened her with all sorts of things—including kicking her out on the street. You've got to understand—that little room in the hospital was practically the only home Jane had known for decades. She would have done anything to keep it. She told Simmons everything—including where the money was coming from." Andrew shook his head again in anger this time. "Damn bastard! He's a mean sod, he is."

"But what did he do about it? I mean if Madame Grazianni was dead…what could anyone do?"

"Oh, she wasn't dead, yet."

Things began to fall into place and my heart dropped. My sweet baby was out there somewhere with a suspected murderer, and I could do nothing about it.

"But…but you really think he killed the old lady?"

"He went to visit Millicent—to see why she'd quit sending the money. And I don't know for sure, but I'd be willing to bet the reason was that she knew Poole was dead and wasn't afraid of him anymore. Joiner thinks William must have gotten furious when she refused to pay up and killed her in a rage with Billy's scissors."

CHAPTER FORTY-FIVE

I was a nervous wreck by the time we pulled up in the Pelican's parking lot. Andrew got out and went inside to inquire if Cassie had been there when we couldn't see any sign of them outside. I would have gone, too; but I was afraid my shaking knees wouldn't hold me up.

It was colder—much colder than it had been when we first left, but my shivering had nothing to do with the temperature. I was scared—terrified of what my sweet Cassie might be going through.

Logically thinking, William had no reason to harm her. He really did not have—or at least I didn't think he had—a reason to suspect we knew what he'd been up to, so why would he want to hurt her? But then on the other hand if he had gotten any inkling that Andy had been watching him and was closing in—he could be using her as a hostage—or worse, a shield.

Even though it was against the law, most everyone around here had police scanners in their cars. I didn't, but then I had a close relationship with Andy. I could always call him and get some idea of what was going on around town, but if William had one and it was tuned to the right frequency, he would know what was coming and where to hide.

Andrew came back outside looking grim and slightly green in the light of the big mercury lamps overhead. He opened the door and climbed in the SUV.

"The good news is that they were here—had dinner, actually, but they left about an hour ago."

"Where…?"

"Dunno. One of the waitresses said she heard them talking about driving over the dam and looking at the lights. So I guess we head that way."

"Which dam?"

"What do you mean 'which' dam? There's only one, right?"

"No! No. There's two—Kentucky Lake and Barkley Lake."

"Bloody oath!" he cursed. "Which one's closer?"

"Kentucky. Not very far from here at all."

Andrew's tires kicked up about half a bucket of gravel as he took off like a jack rabbit. He swung out to the highway and turned left, flinging me against the car door. In response, I tightened up my seat belt and hung on for dear life. Andrew was on a mission to rescue Cassie, and I was with him all the way.

"Thanks for not holding a grudge."

He glanced quickly at me and smothered a nervous laugh. "Too right! She does think I'm a piker, doesn't she!"

"Well, maybe…"

"Never mind, I know just what she thinks of me. And she's right. I did behave badly. Very badly, as a matter of fact; but I had a reason, at least to my crazy way of thinking."

"Which was?" I asked, as my eyes quickly took in all the passing cars. I had assumed that William would be driving the same one he had come to dinner in—a light grey SUV with over-sized tires, but his sister might have a vehicle, too. He might have used Sandy's for the date with Cassie—in which case I had no idea what to look for, except one with two people in the front seat. And that was only about every other car.

"Didn't want her to really fall for me," he announced, self-importantly.

I couldn't stop the laughter, nor the comment that should have stayed unsaid.

"No chance of that!"

"Wow! Way to hurt a bloke. I'm not exactly a bluger, you know. I'm aces in Oz. Some sheilas would consider…"

"Wait," I cried. "There's his car—parked over there by the lock."

"Lock? And you talk about not understanding my language!"

"The lock! The lock that lets barges and boats go across the dam—from the lake to the river!"

Andrew slowed down abruptly and turned around at the nearest wide spot in the road. He headed back towards the little park where tourists could leave their cars while they climbed up the hill to watch river traffic traverse the dam.

At my direction, he pulled into the drive and parked behind the huge turbine which sat in the middle to remind visitors of what the dam created—electricity, from the turbines just like this one, inside the enormous structure.

He turned off the headlights and we sat still until our eyes adjusted to the darkness. William's SUV sat at the end of the lot, but Cassie and William were nowhere to be seen.

CHAPTER FORTY-SIX

The moon hid behind wintery clouds, obscuring everything on land. The night air had a chilly edge to it, and I wondered vaguely if we were going to have an early snow.

"Do you see anything?"

The dam stretched out across the lake in front of us wearing a string of lights like a diamond necklace. The reflection shimmered in the waves created from the water coming out of the one open spillway. On any other night and under any other circumstances I would have thought it a beautiful sight—the creative combination of man and nature. But tonight I was too terrified to think about anything but my daughter's welfare.

I had ignored Andrew's question while I searched for any movement around us, but I didn't see a thing, and neither, I was certain, did he.

"I'm going up that hill," he announced, pointing to the concrete steps that led up the hill and into the darkness beyond. "Maybe they're up there."

"And what are we going to do if we find them? And I mean 'we' because I'm right behind you." I hesitated for a moment. "Maybe this is the time we should call Andy and let him know where we are."

He shook his head. I could barely see him in the light reflected from the dam. But I could tell from the stern set of his face that he had no intention of waiting for anyone. A man after my own heart, I thought.

"Let's go then," I urged. "But stick to what little cover there is and try to stay in the shadows."

"Don't worry," he chuckled. "What is it your cowboys say? 'This ain't my first rodeo.'"

"Oh, really?"

"Well, yeah, it is, but I've just always wanted to say that."

I patted his shoulder reassuringly and opened the door. "Good luck, Hopalong."

We crept around the car and hid behind the huge monument to the TVA project that had brought this system of dams to the area over sixty years ago—alleviating the terrible floods that had destroyed towns and farms for years.

Whole settlements had been moved to higher ground to make room for the dam and somewhere beneath the dark waters abandoned homes and churches waited silently while they slowly decayed and filled with muck and algae.

I shook off the feeling of dread and welcomed the rush of fear that made my heart beat faster as it prepared my body for flight or fight. I was ready for whatever it took to rescue my baby.

"Well, hi, Mom! What in the world are you doing here?"

Andrew and I turned around at the same time and painfully butted heads. I staggered back and shook off the blackness and stars that flashed before my eyes. Cassie was here—looking alive and well—and completely at ease.

"Bloody hell…?"

"Huntley, what are you doing sneaking around spying on me with my mom?"

"It's okay, Cassie. We're not spying, we're …well, I don't exactly know what we're doing, but it's for your own good. I promise you that."

"Right you are, love. We're here to…wait just a minute! Where is Simmons? Where is your, eh, date?"

"Right here," William answered as he stepped out from behind the monument. "I had a phone call from my sister. "What's going on?"

The moon chose that moment to come out from behind a cloud and illuminate William's face. He looked worried and upset, and I knew his sister had called to warn him about the police. Andrew knew it, too, because he reached in his jacket pocket and pulled out a nasty little gun and pointed it straight at William's head.

CHAPTER FORTY-SEVEN

"Hey, wait a minute," I protested. "We didn't say anything about bringing guns to the party. What do you think you're doing?"

Andrew ignored my question and took a step closer to William. "Come over here, Cassie. Get behind me," he ordered.

"Why…why should I?" she stammered, her face pale in the moonlight. "Mom, what's this all about? Why is Huntley acting so weird?"

"Tell her! Tell her what her fancy-man date has been up to, why don't you, Paisley. Tell her about the money he stole from my Aunt Jane, and by all means tell her about how he murdered that poor old woman in cold blood!"

"Mom?"

"Do what he says, honey. Come over here by me."

"I think not," William's voice was harsh and stilted. "She's coming with me."

"I'm not going anywhere with anybody until somebody tells me what this is all about," declared my daughter.

"Oh, I think you will," Sandy Simmons uttered in a soft but deadly voice as she stepped out of the shadows. "I guess this is what they call a 'Mexican stand-off,'" she laughed, as she pointed an equally deadly weapon at Cassie's head. "Now, drop the gun and move it up that hill or I'll shoot all three of you right here."

"Sandy! Why didn't you let me take care of this like I told you I would?"

"Ha! Like you 'took care' of the old lady? Fat lot of good that 'little talking to' did for us. She deserved to die, and you know it. We needed that money, William. I don't know why you went so soft on those two old crones. If you'd listened to me in the first place we could have gotten that old woman committed and slowly bled her dry just like we have all the others. Instead, I had to teach her a lesson. I've been behind you two every minute since you left home. I knew I'd have to step in and take over like I always have."

She reached out and grabbed Cassie's arm. I could tell she was leaving a bruise from the way Cassie winced. I started forward, but Andrew held me back. "Not now, Paisley," he whispered, as our little party slowly began climbing the concrete steps up the hill to the observation platform.

I searched the horizon for any sign of Andy Joiner and his troops, but I couldn't see any flashing lights on the road. It looked like Andrew and I had truly botched things up and it was Cassie who would pay the price.

We reached the wide concrete apron overlooking the lock in short order. Below were the huge gates that opened and closed to raise or lower the water level between river and lake to allow passage of barges and boats from one to the other.

As we watched, the big gates slowly closed at one end and the water began to rise in the lock. Sure enough, on the other side about a quarter of a mile away I could see the vague outline of a coal barge slowly making its way down the river.

The sound of the opening of the valves and the rushing water made it almost impossible to be heard. Sandy motioned, instead, with the point of her gun and left no question about what it was she wanted us to do.

"No bloody way, are we going to jump over the side," shouted Andrew. "You're nuts, lady! Bonkers!"

She was fast for such a plump little woman, and Andrew didn't have to time to duck. The gun hit him in the temple and he dropped like a rock to the ground. I knelt swiftly and felt for Andrew's pulse. I found, one—a weak one, but there it was—at least for the time being.

"For goodness sakes!" I cried. You don't have to kill us, too! The police are on to you—well, at least they are on to William. They'll be here any minute. I know! I heard Andrew speaking to Joiner about it."

Sandy's voice sounded smug when she answered. "I know. I heard it, too. But they're going in the wrong direction—to the wrong dam. We'll be over this little unpleasantness here before they ever figure it out. And William and I will be halfway to Mexico and points south before they find your bodies in the filth and mire underneath these waters. God bless the TVA!"

CHAPTER FORTY-EIGHT

Cassie stepped over closer to my side, but I pushed her gently away. She looked scared and hurt, but when I made my move I didn't want her in the way. I knew I would have to rush the crazy woman in front of me, and I also knew that probably meant a bullet in the gut. But I would do anything to keep Cassie safe.

When Sandy urged us onto the ledge above the lock, I stepped out and in front of Cassie. Sandy stood just to my right holding her little gun so tightly her knuckles shone like little white knobs in the moonlight. I realized then that she was scared…almost as scared as I was, but she thought she had the upper hand. I was counting on that—certain that she would be completely taken by surprise if I rushed her. And I prayed that she would not have time to pull the trigger.

I braced myself for what surely would be the worst pain of my life, and took a quick last look at my sweet baby's face. But before I could take that step to knock Sandy Simmons off her feet and into the dark waters below, Andrew Alesworthy charged past me and plowed into her dumpy little body and over the side.

"Sandy!"

I made the most of William's shock and horror by grabbing the gun out of his hand. He ran to the ledge and cried out for his sister. When he saw she was well and truly lost in the dark swirling rush of water below, he fell on the ground and sobbed. I made the most of the situation by grabbing Cassie's silk scarf and tying his hands behind his back. Overcome by distress, he made no move to stop me.

"Oh, Mom!"

I hugged my daughter tighter than I ever had. She felt good and warm and alive. And I was so thankful I almost fell on my own knees right then and there.

"Poor Huntley!" she sobbed. "He saved our lives, you know?" Her beautiful face was streaked with tears, and I could feel mine starting. Andrew had, indeed, saved our lives.

"Joiner's here," I announced, my voice a bit muffled by her shoulder. "I'd better get you to his car. Maybe he has some blankets and some hot coffee. Don't want you going into shock."

"Oh, pooh! I'm not some withering little violet, you know. I'm just cold."

Andy Joiner loped up the stairs three at a time and had William in handcuffs, before a shivering Cassie and I had wrapped ourselves in the blankets his deputies brought us. We all made a slow little procession back down to the waiting cruisers—their lights flashing blue and red in the parking lot. Andy had indeed brought lots of hot coffee and he poured us some while he asked the inevitable questions.

"What the hell did you two think you were doing?"

"Mmm, Andy…"

"Does anything I ever say get through to you?"

"But, Andy…"

"Didn't I warn you about this guy?"

"I didn't think…"

"That's the problem!"

CHAPTER FORTY-NINE

Mother and Horatio came home that same evening. They almost left again when Andy started yelling at Horatio about controlling the females under his roof. And that made me mad enough to throw off the Lakeland County issue blanket and tell him I was going to tell his wife and daughters that he was a Neanderthal—a throwback to the "little missy stays in the kitchen days." And they would take care of him, in no uncertain terms!

Before long we were all yelling and then the tears started again—first with Cassie, then Mother and finally me. Horatio glared at Andy for bringing all this about and Andy confessed he was just so darned scared when he heard he had gone to the wrong place. He was sure he would arrive too late to save us. And he started sniffing suspiciously.

Horatio took the floor and declared all was well and forgiven and settled himself in his chair by the fire for a long overdue pipe. Mother broke out the wonderful little British tea cakes she had brought as souvenirs from the islands and Cassie made us some more hot coffee.

Andy didn't stay long. He got a call right in the middle of our little tea party that made him jump up and run out the door with only a cursory farewell. I was curious, but not curious enough to give up a hot shower and a warm bed.

Cassie slept with me that night.

Horatio had gone to pick up a seeming recovered Aggie early in the morning and she crept into my room and slept between us like a real dog and not the vicious little vixen she was.

When Mother finally tapped gently on my door at noon the next day, I groaned and turned over—not knowing that Aggie was there. I felt the bite all the way through the blankets, quilt, and down comforter.

"Damn dog!"

"Really, Paisley! Do try and act more like a lady for once," whispered Mother. "We have company, and I don't want them to think you're a total barbarian."

"Then get that little blankity blank beast off my bed! Damn that hurt! And who in the hell comes to visit so early in the morning?"

She smiled brightly and held the door while Aggie marched smartly out—her morning duties done by spoiling my day.

"It's not that early, dear, and besides—I think it's someone you'll be very happy to see." And with that cryptic remark she closed the door and left.

Since I'd had my shower the night before, I threw on a faded old sweatshirt and some jeans—brushed my teeth, tried to brush my hair, and slipped on my loafers. And all this was while Cassie slept peacefully.

I heard voices in the kitchen before I got halfway down the hall. One voice in particular stood out, but I couldn't believe my ears until I rounded the corner and saw Andrew Alesworthy in the flesh—or rather—flesh, cast and bandages.

"Huntley!" I shouted. "My God! You're alive!"

He tried to stand, but the crutch he had under his one good arm slipped on the kitchen floor and wincing, he plopped back down in the chair.

"Of course, I am. I'm tougher than a boomer. Can't kill me."

"Well, they certainly made a good try," quipped Andy Joiner. "If it hadn't been for that coal barge coming through the lock when it did…"

"What happened?" I interrupted. "And where's Sandy Simmons? Did she land on the barge, too?"

"Well, almost," admitted Andy. "Her head hit the corner and she fell back in the water. The divers from coast guard are still searching for her body this morning."

"So…"

"So, she's dead, Paisley. And William is in the cell that Billy has occupied for the last couple of months. And before you open your mouth—he's free as a bird with all the apologies the city of Rowan Springs can offer."

"Thank God for that," I sighed as I sank down in a chair next to Andrew. "Then it's all over?"

"All over," said Andy with a nod. "Except for all the legalese—the charges, the trial, and the sentencing. William has accrued a whole bunch of charges. It'll take a month of Sundays to figure all of them out, considering it's back and forth from one country to another. The good news is that Miss Mary Jane Alesworthy—Andrew's aunt will most likely be exonerated because of her mental status. And he's offered to let her come live with him so he can watch over her himself."

"Why, Hunt…Andrew, dear," offered Mother, "that's lovely of you. The dear old thing sounds like such a lovely woman. I'd like to meet her sometime. Maybe she can…"

"Maybe you can come and meet her sometime—in her new establishment," announced Andrew rather grandly.

"And that would be?" asked Cassie, yawning from the doorway.

"Why, hello, Cassie, love," said Andrew softly. "That would be at the opening of the brand new purveyor of Aussie-style shrimp on the barbie in Minton on the lake. It's going to be called 'Mad Queen Jane's.'"

CHAPTER FIFTY

We all relaxed for the next few days and did nothing but eat and sleep and enjoy each other's company. Cassie was still a little shell-shocked, and I was beginning to wonder about my people-picker being a bit off. What was the matter with my intuition? Where had I gone wrong in thinking William was 'Mr. Butter Don't Melt In His Mouth,' and Andrew was a nefarious villain? The only one who appeared to have flown beneath my radar was Mick, and we saw a lot of him that winter.

It was fun having someone around who had no agenda. He was as uncomplicated and unsophisticated as the country his 'oldies' had come from. And we all enjoyed his 'bonzer' tales of the land down under—whether they were true or not. One tale in particular interested me. Seems a brumby got caught in some wire fencing—something not often used on a station, but this time a rancher, or station master, had been making a pen for his son's new puppies. The pen was not to keep the puppies in, but to keep the dingoes out.

The brumby reared up and fought the fence until he was well and truly entangled with the barbed wire. The barbs cut deep and cruelly, causing the poor animal to scream in pain. Like all good Aussie station masters, this one had a storehouse of meds to care for the various animals under his roof, so to speak—and he pulled out some local anesthesia to calm the horse so his men could cut him loose.

Only problem was he used too much on the horse's stomach and ears—where the hide was thin and the anesthetic got into the bloodstream quicker and in greater amounts. The poor beast faltered and died before they could free him. Seems the anesthetic used in great amounts thinned the blood, among other things, and the horse bled to death in front of them.

It was a sad tale, and Cassie was almost in tears before it was over; but it got me thinking.

The night Aggie had been near death in Andrew's surgery, he had shaved a small spot on her little tummy, donned some heavy rubber gloves, and rubbed in a very small amount of anesthetic 'to help relieve the pain in her belly,' he had said. When I asked how it worked, he quickly told me about the transdermal vehicle vets used to get meds into animals who couldn't swallow pills. It had some long chemical name which didn't register at all, but I remembered the acronym: DMSO.

Mick's story had made me curious, so I did some research on the drug and quickly found an article about a drug company in Brisbane. The Australian company had been fined and their license taken away for unlawfully using a 'schedule 4 poison'—DMSO— in one of their topical medications.

Apparently this particular 'schedule 4 poison,' increased the effects of blood thinners, heart medications, and steroids—sometimes with fatal results. There was even a supposition that it had caused the death of a woman after topical use for a ligament sprain. And all this excitement took place around the time a bright young university student would have studied it as a cautionary tale.

It kinda made you want to go, "hmmm."

CHAPTER FIFTY-ONE

I finally got up the nerve to confront Andrew about my suspicions one spring day when I went back to Minton. The reason for my trip was to check out the new restaurant's menu before the grand opening the next day.

Everything was delicious, and I told the proud new owners so. "Especially your shrimp, Mick! Where in the world did you find such colossal shrimp?"

"Trade secret, love," he answered proudly. "If I told you, I'd have to kill you."

"Um, speaking of that, do you mind if I have a word with Andrew alone?"

Mick looked puzzled for a moment, and then the penny dropped. With apologies to the others, he took me off to one side.

"That would be okay, except maybe I'm the one you want to speak to, not Andrew."

"Mick—surely not you?"

"Not admitting to a thing, Paisley, and please don't bring this up to Andrew. He's been through enough for one lifetime."

"But…"

He sat down heavily in the chair next to me.

"Funny, isn't it? I never met Andrew until this year but I knew about him all my life. Aunt Jane was very proud of him—bragged about him all the time. When she told me about her little blackmail scheme over the years, I didn't believe her—considering her background of mental illness and all—but six months ago when she asked me to empty out her bank account and invest what was left for the future…"

"So that's how you and Andrew managed to buy the restaurant?"

"Yeah, and to take care of her, too. She really is a grand old lady, she is. And Andrew and I are all she's got. It would kill her to lose either one of us, Paisley. Think about that, will you, when you decide what to do about a hateful old pervert's death—a hateful old man who never gave up on his addiction to—"

"Never mind, you don't have to draw me a picture."

"But there *were* pictures, Paisley—hundreds of pictures—even some old faded ones of Jane, and Millicent, and Meg watching the awful things he did to those two little girls. But most of them were of other young girls—many, many young girls being abused and degraded and ruined just like he did his own daughters."

He was crying silently now, the big shiny tears rolling down his cheeks into the soft downy beard.

"He had to be stopped, Paisley, love. The pictures had to be destroyed. You do see that, don't you?"

I remained quiet. What could I say?

"I remembered the story about the rancher and the brumby, and it was easy enough to glom onto some of that medicine when I went on a tour of Andrew's new office. He was so proud of being able to find a way back to Rowan Springs. He wanted to do the right thing—the thing his mum had raised him to do—but he just couldn't go through with it. And mind you now, I'm not saying I did it, but it's a sure thing that no one will ever miss the likes of a monster like James A. Poole."

* * * *

I drove home slowly. The events of the day tried to find a comfortable place to settle down in my mind—like Aggie circling the sofa cushion before she took her nap. I was still mulling over the things I had learned when I pulled up in the driveway of the big old house on Meadowdale Farm.

Cassie was out front gathering up the first daffodils of the season in a big wicker basket—no doubt for a dinner table bouquet. Aggie was running circles around her mistress, trying to get her to go for a romp, and Horatio and Mother, all bundled up in sweaters, were enjoying what was surely the first of many evenings on the patio.

The closeness of my loving family brought forth memories of how my parents and grandparents thought—what their values were and how they really felt about their fellow man.

I was lucky. They were good people—people who were not just socially kind, but truly kind—especially when no one was looking. I was proud of them, and even as a small child I had known I was in the midst of something very special. Once, when I was five and it suddenly occurred to me that I was very lucky to be loved by these extraordinary folk, I started crying—overcome with emotion.

When my grandmother asked what was wrong, I cheapened the moment by declaring the big boys up the street had thrown rocks at me, and then slunk off to my room, ashamed of my lie; ashamed that I couldn't bring myself to tell them how much I loved them, not for fear of being rejected, but fear of sounding fey. Love was never in short supply in our house, but it was never mentioned. I wasn't prepared at the age of five to change the pattern. I saved that for after Cassie was born—and I've told her I love her every day since.

I couldn't help but feel that what Andrew had intended to do—and what Mick had done—was done out of love…and a desire to set things right with a sometimes wonky universe. Suddenly I felt at peace with what I had learned and what I would forget, and went to join the people who loved me as much as I loved them.